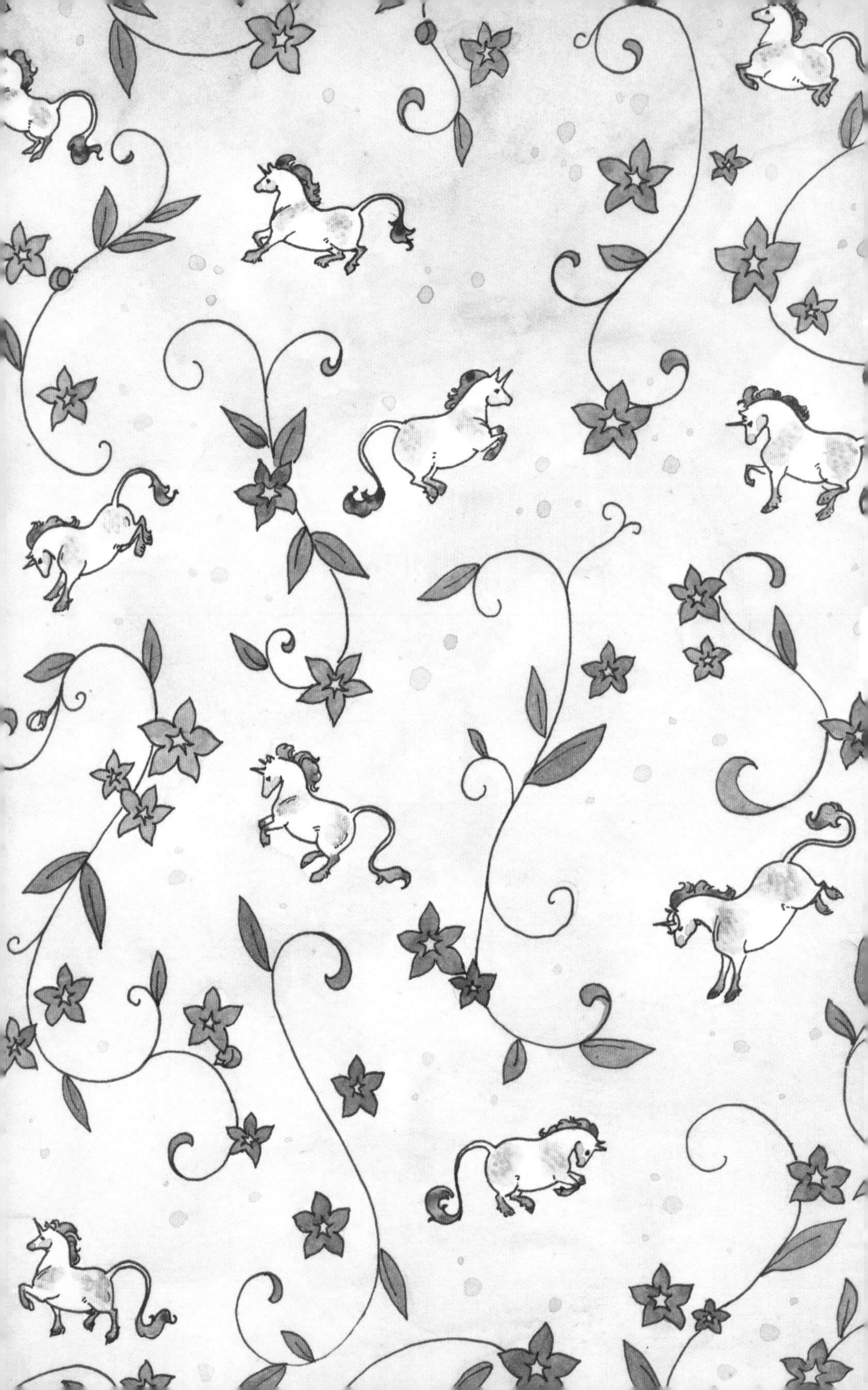

EMILINE
Knight in Training

AN ONI PRESS PUBLICATION

EMILINE
Knight in Training

By Kimberli Johnson
Lettered by Crank!

Edited by **Ari Yarwood**
Designed by **Kate Z. Stone**

onipress.com
facebook.com/onipress
twitter.com/onipress
onipress.tumblr.com
instagram.com/onipress

kimberlistudio.com
twitter.com/Kimberlistudio
instagram.com/kimberlistudio

Lettered using OpenDyslexic

First Edition: July 2019
ISBN 978-1-62010-644-0
eISBN 978-1-62010-645-7

Emiline: Knight in Training, July 2019. Published by Oni Press, Inc. 1319 SE Martin Luther King Jr. Blvd., Suite 240, Portland, OR 97214.

Printed in China.

Library of Congress Control Number: 2018967178

1 3 5 7 9 10 8 6 4 2

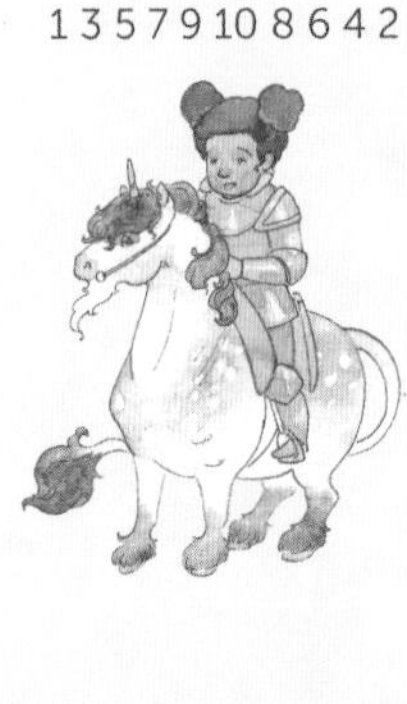

Published by Oni Press, Inc.

Joe Nozemack
Founder & Chief Financial Officer

James Lucas Jones
Publisher

Sarah Gaydos
Editor in Chief

Charlie Chu
V.P. of Creative & Business Development

Brad Rooks
Director of Operations

Melissa Meszaros
Director of Publicity

Margot Wood
Director of Sales

Sandy Tanaka
Marketing Design Manager

Amber O'Neill
Special Projects Manager

Troy Look
Director of Design & Production

Kate Z. Stone
Senior Graphic Designer

Sonja Synak
Graphic Designer

Angie Knowles
Digital Prepress Lead

Robin Herrera
Senior Editor

Ari Yarwood
Senior Editor

Desiree Wilson
Associate Editor

Kate Light
Editorial Assistant

Michelle Nguyen
Executive Assistant

Jung Lee
Logistics Coordinator

To my Mom
and the countless hours she spent
helping me learn to read.

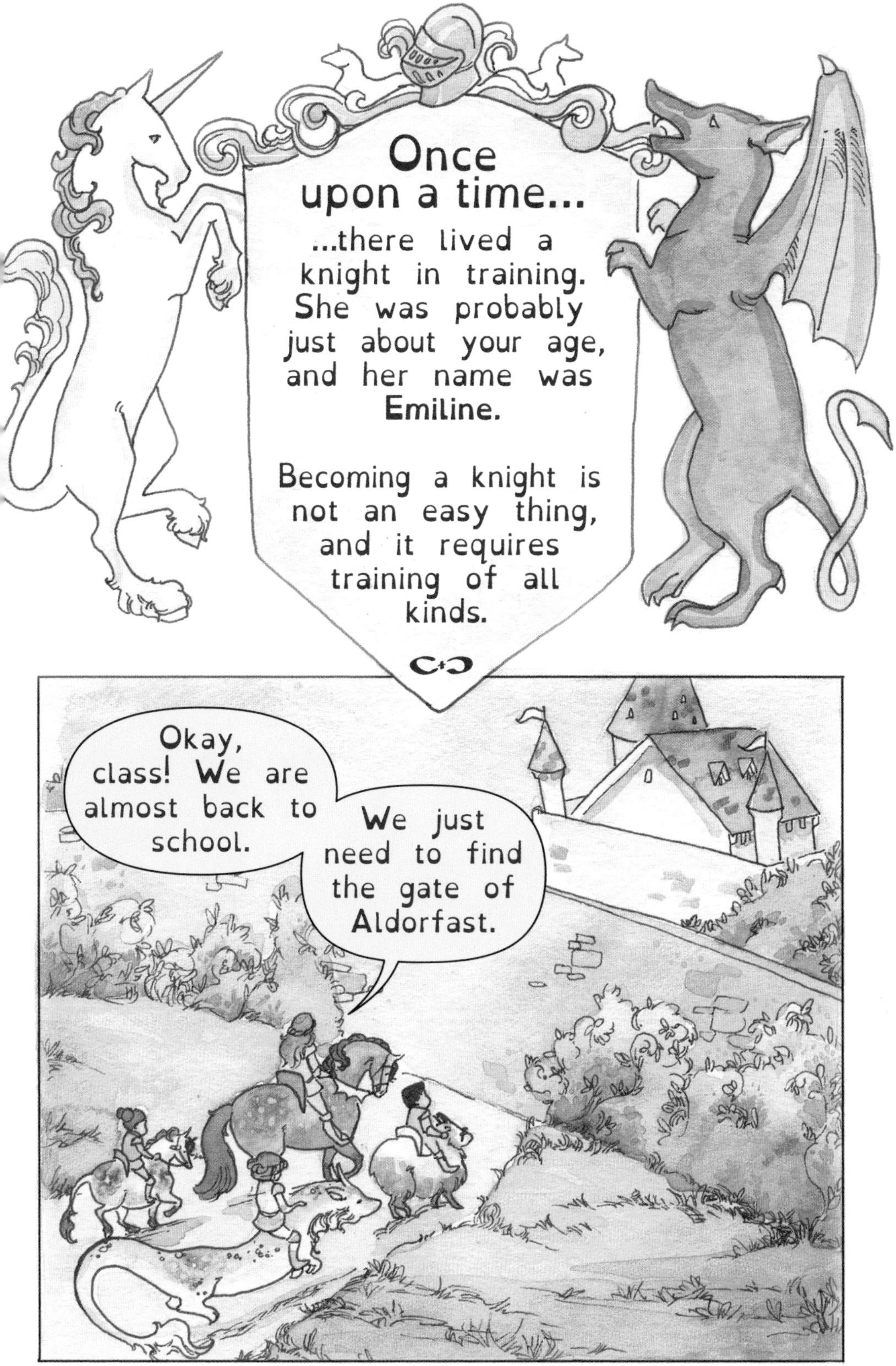
Once upon a time...
...there lived a knight in training. She was probably just about your age, and her name was Emiline.
Becoming a knight is not an easy thing, and it requires training of all kinds.
Okay, class! We are almost back to school.
We just need to find the gate of Aldorfast.

Can enter through the
Look, a handprint!

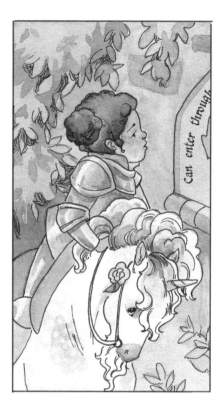

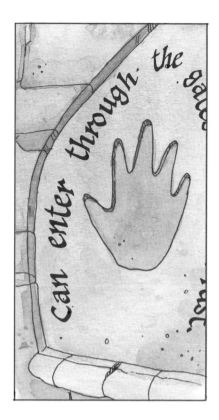

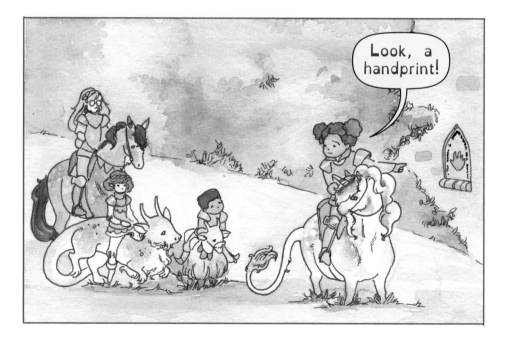

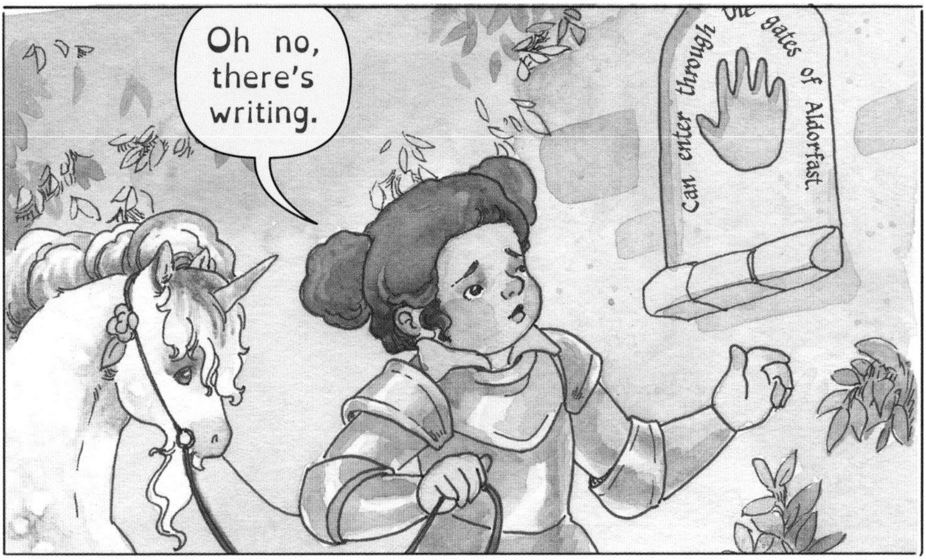
Oh no, there's writing.
Can enter through
gates of Aldorfast.

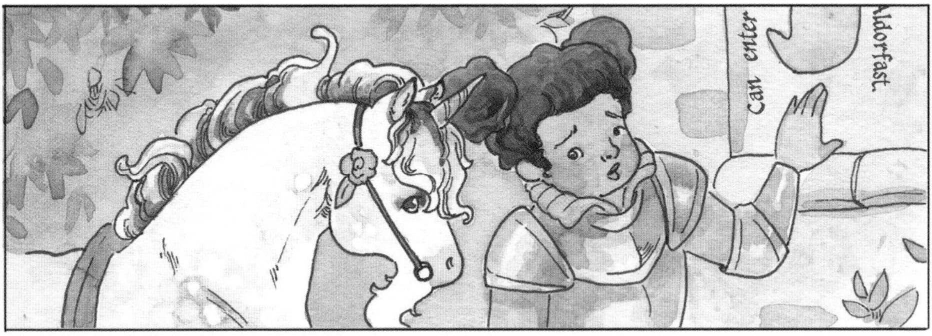
Can enter
Aldorfast.

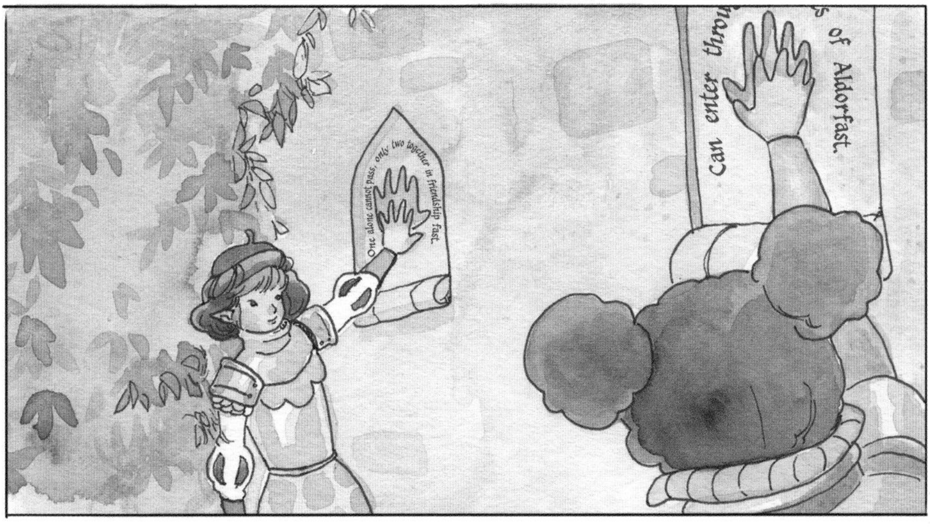
One alone cannot pass, only two together in friendship fast.
Can enter
of Aldorfast.

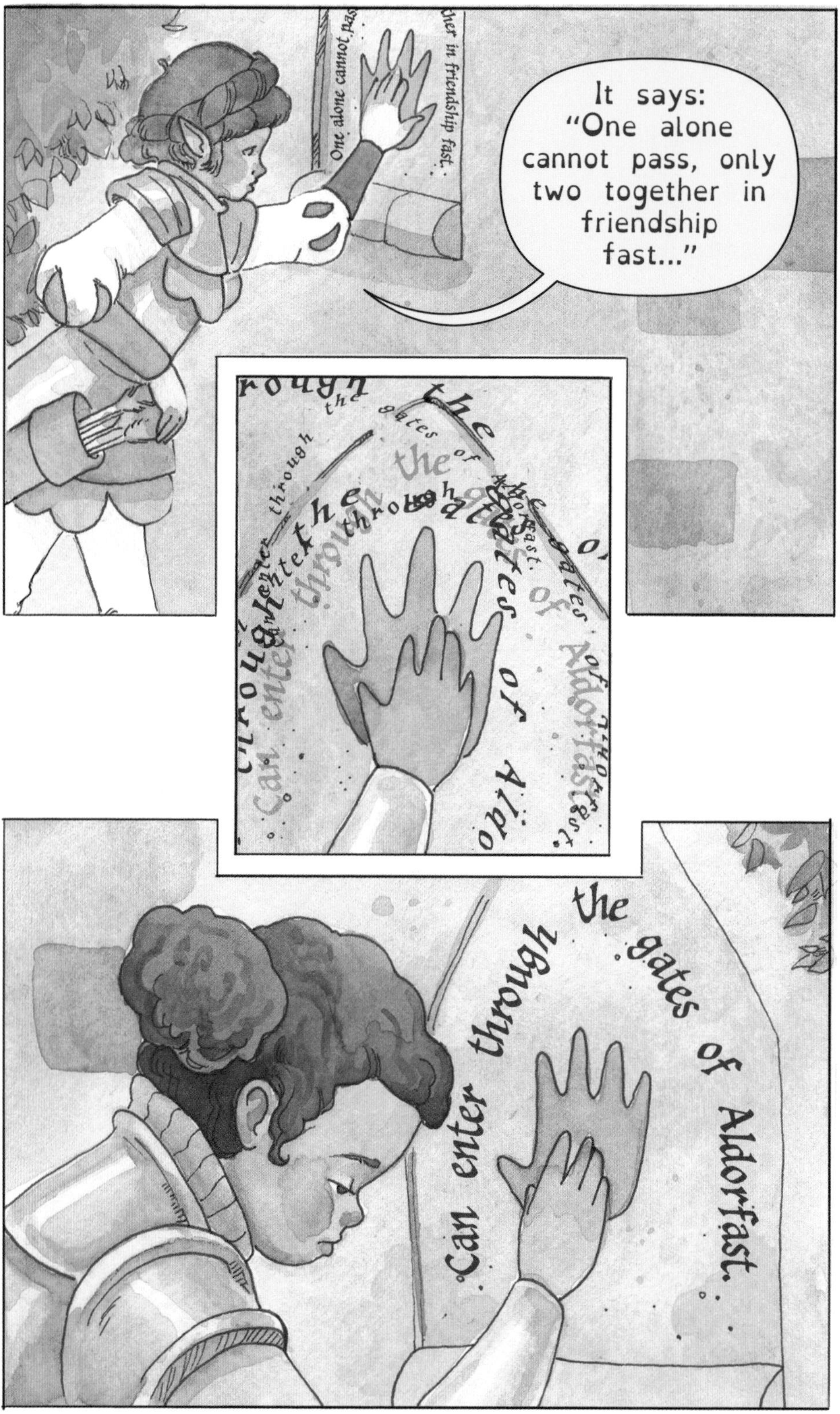
One alone cannot pas
ther in friendship fast.
It says: "One alone cannot pass, only two together in friendship fast..."
Can enter through the gates of Aldorfast.

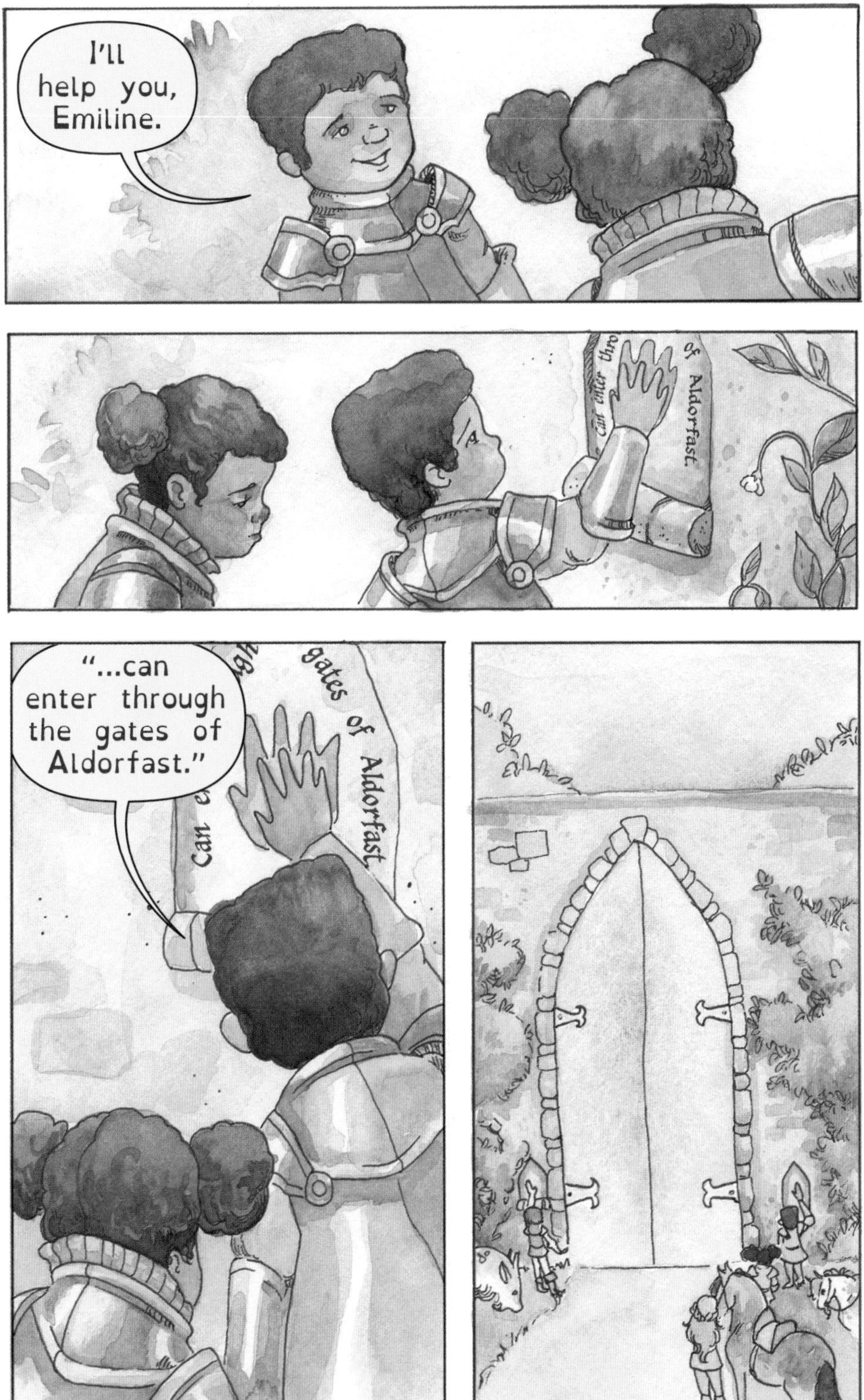
I'll help you, Emiline.
of Aldorfast.
"...can enter through the gates of Aldorfast."
gates of Aldorfast

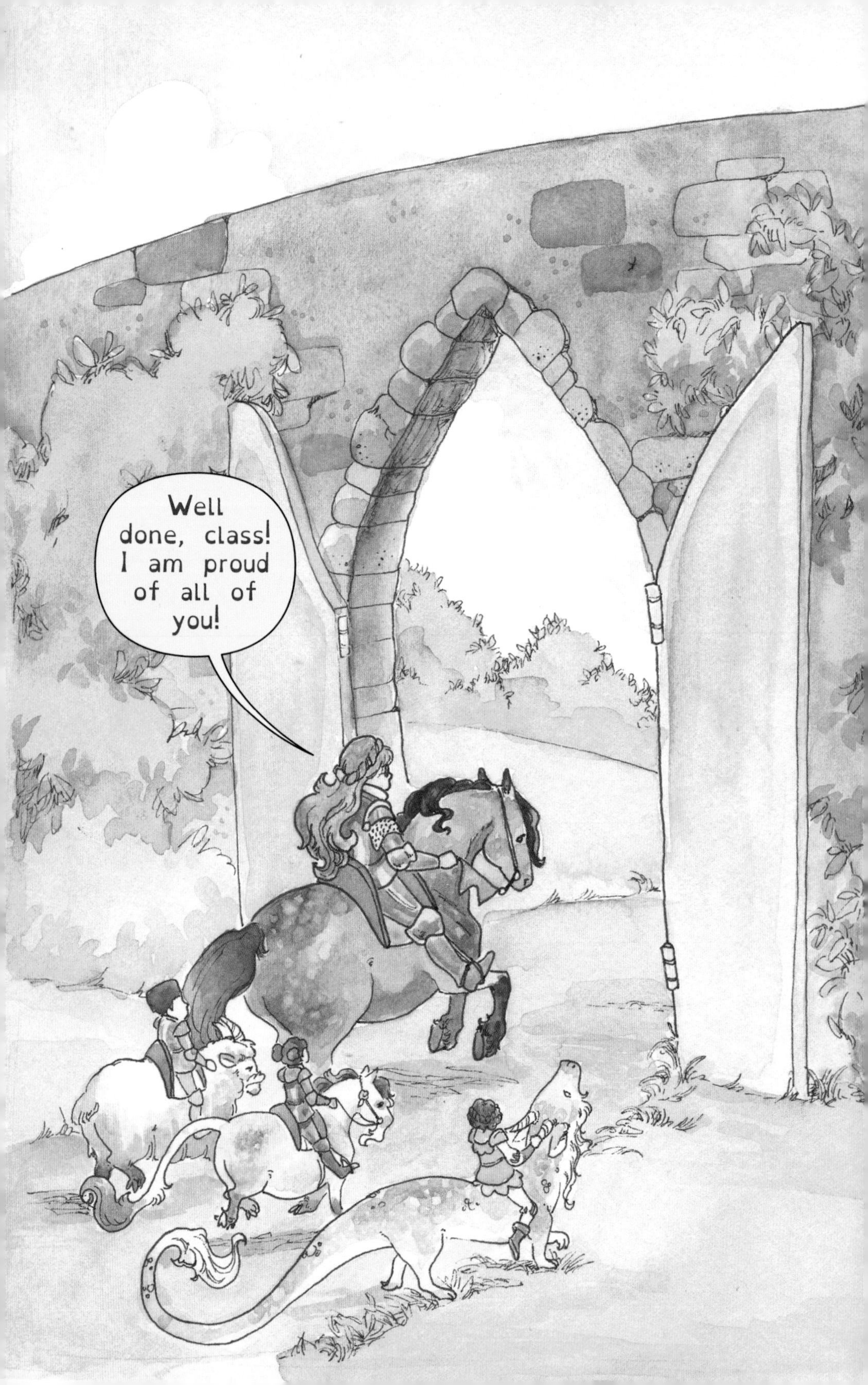
Well done, class! I am proud of all of you!

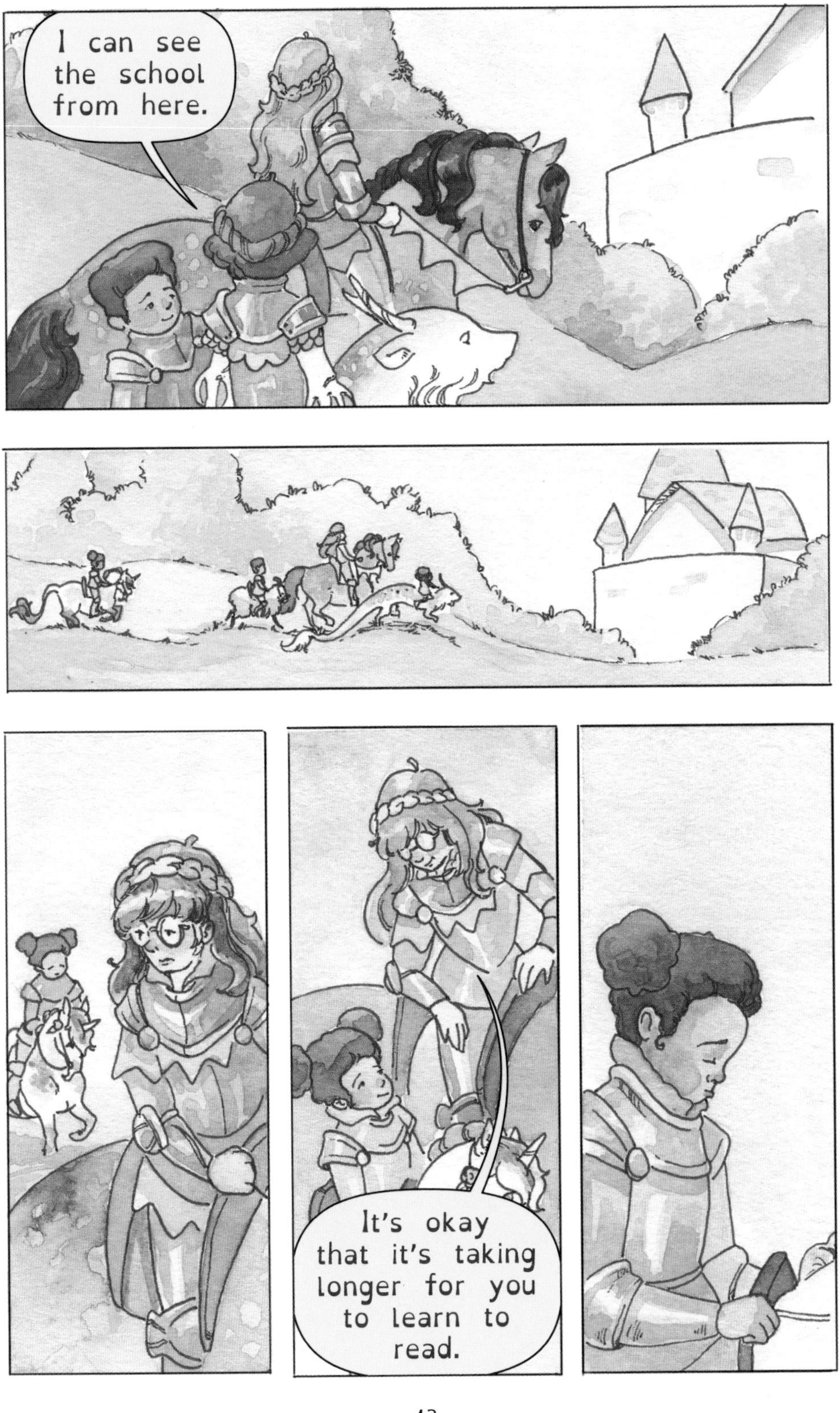
I can see the school from here.
It's okay that it's taking longer for you to learn to read.

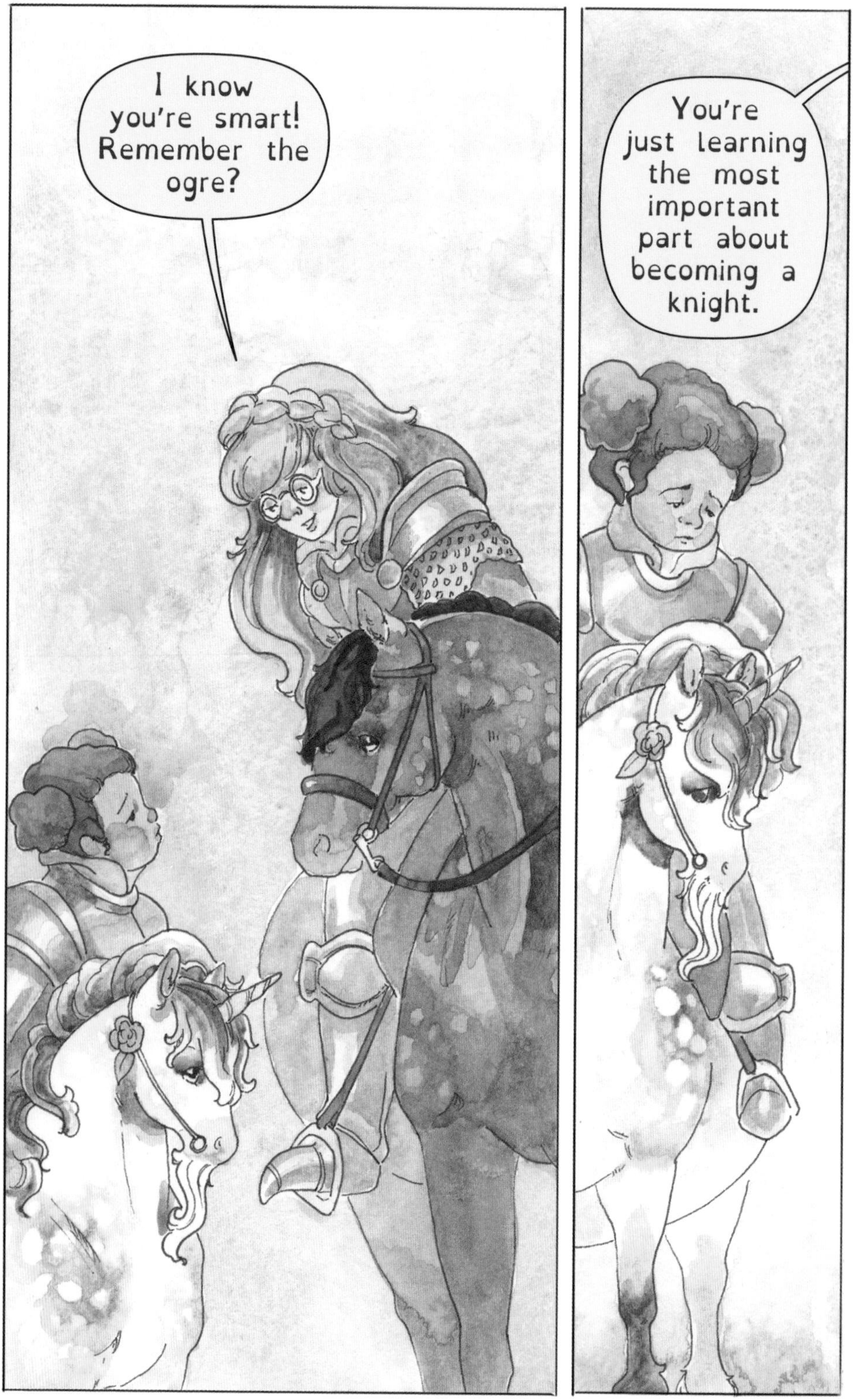
I know you're smart! Remember the ogre?
You're just learning the most important part about becoming a knight.

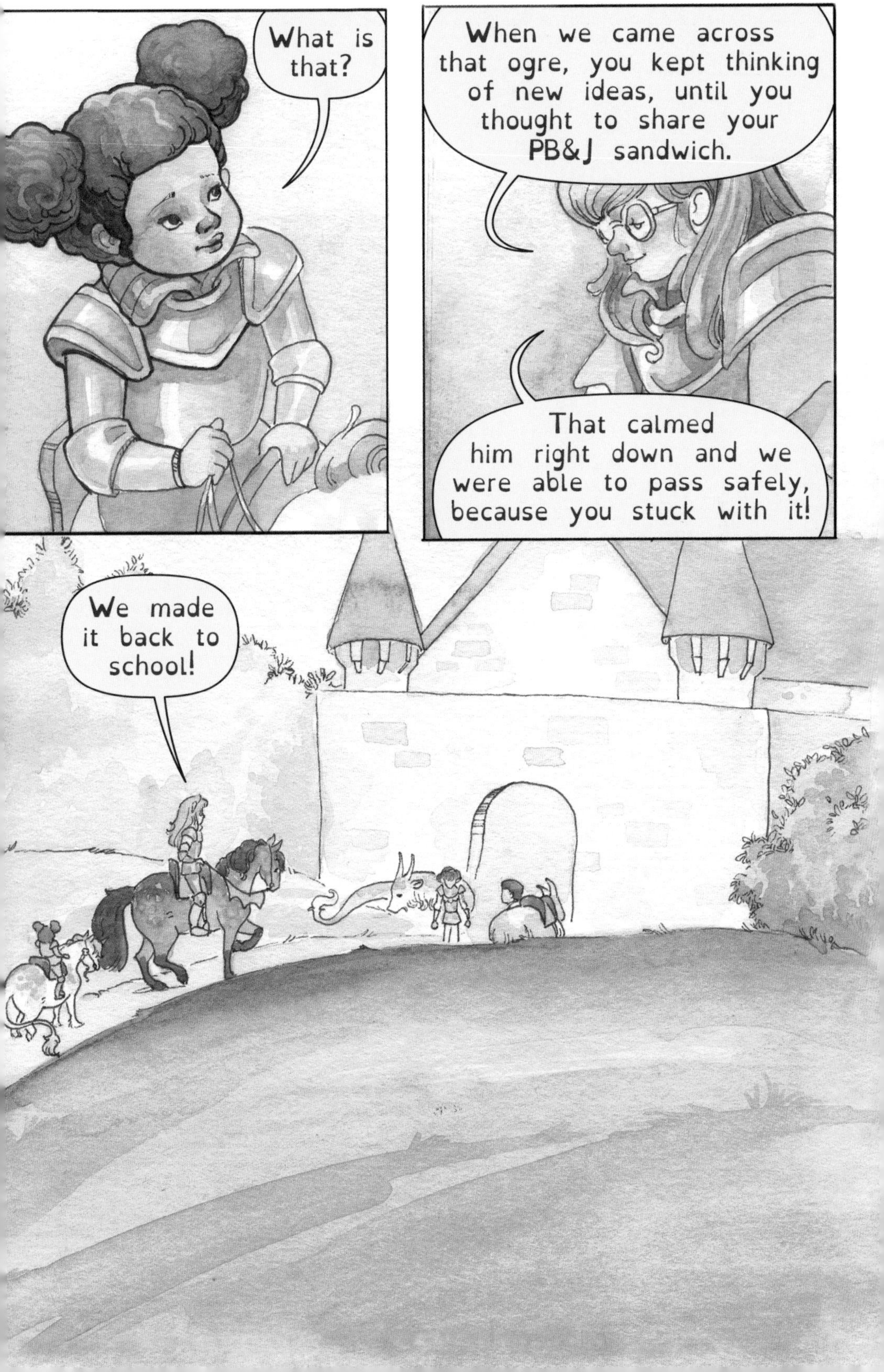
What is that?
When we came across that ogre, you kept thinking of new ideas, until you thought to share your PB&J sandwich.
That calmed him right down and we were able to pass safely, because you stuck with it!
We made it back to school!

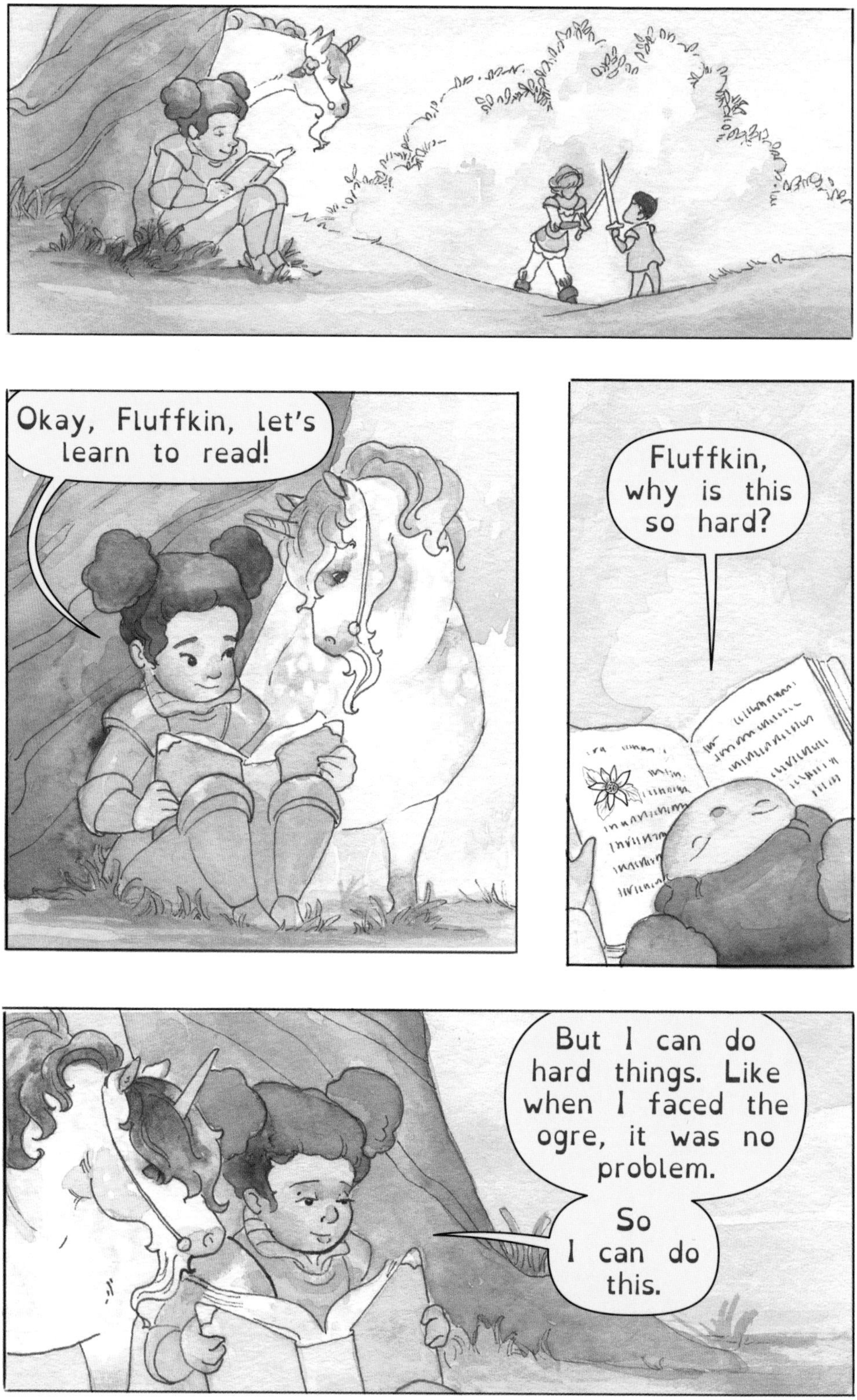
Okay, Fluffkin, let's learn to read!
Fluffkin, why is this so hard?
But I can do hard things. Like when I faced the ogre, it was no problem.
So I can do this.

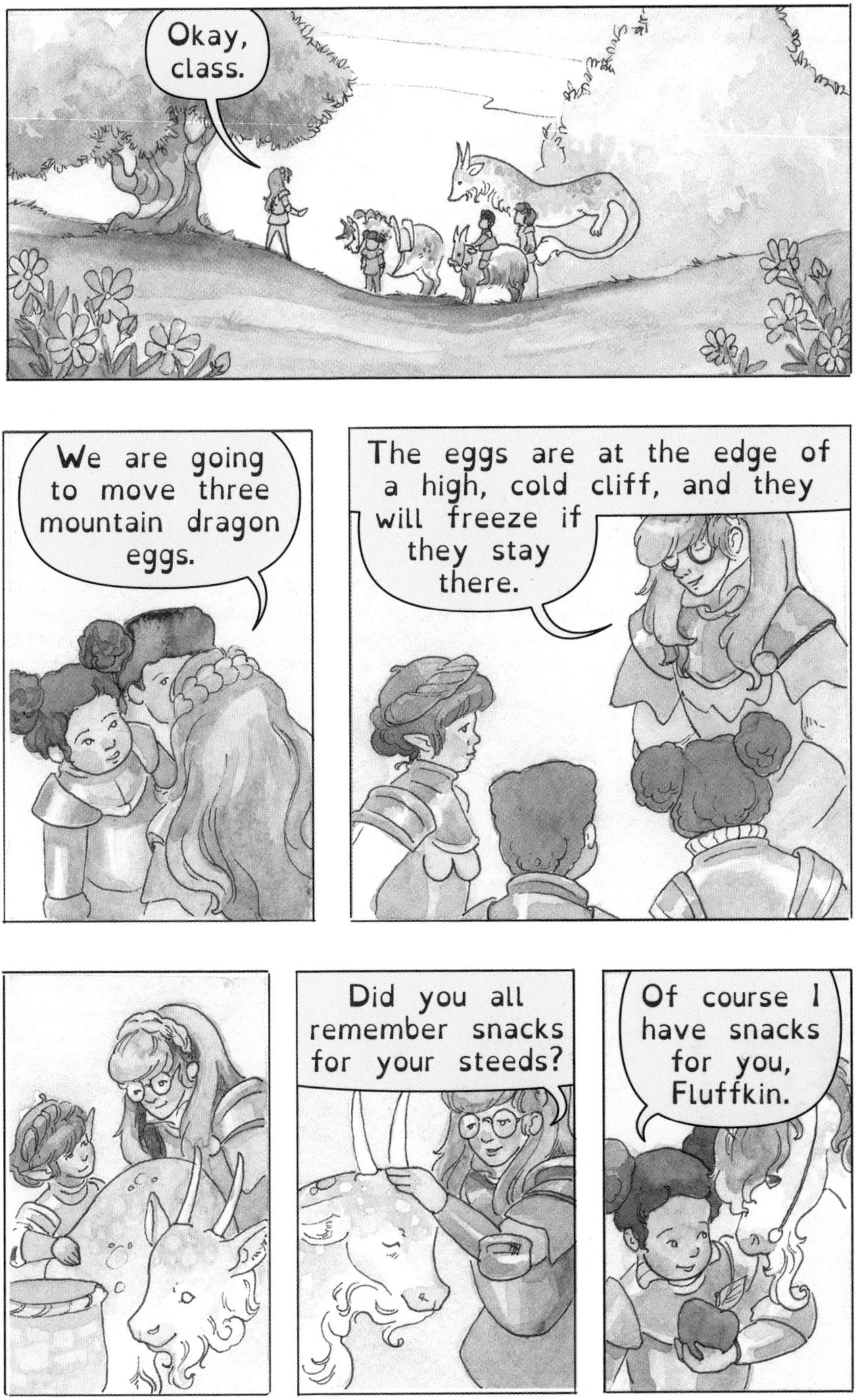
Okay, class.
We are going to move three mountain dragon eggs.
The eggs are at the edge of a high, cold cliff, and they will freeze if they stay there.
Did you all remember snacks for your steeds?
Of course I have snacks for you, Fluffkin.

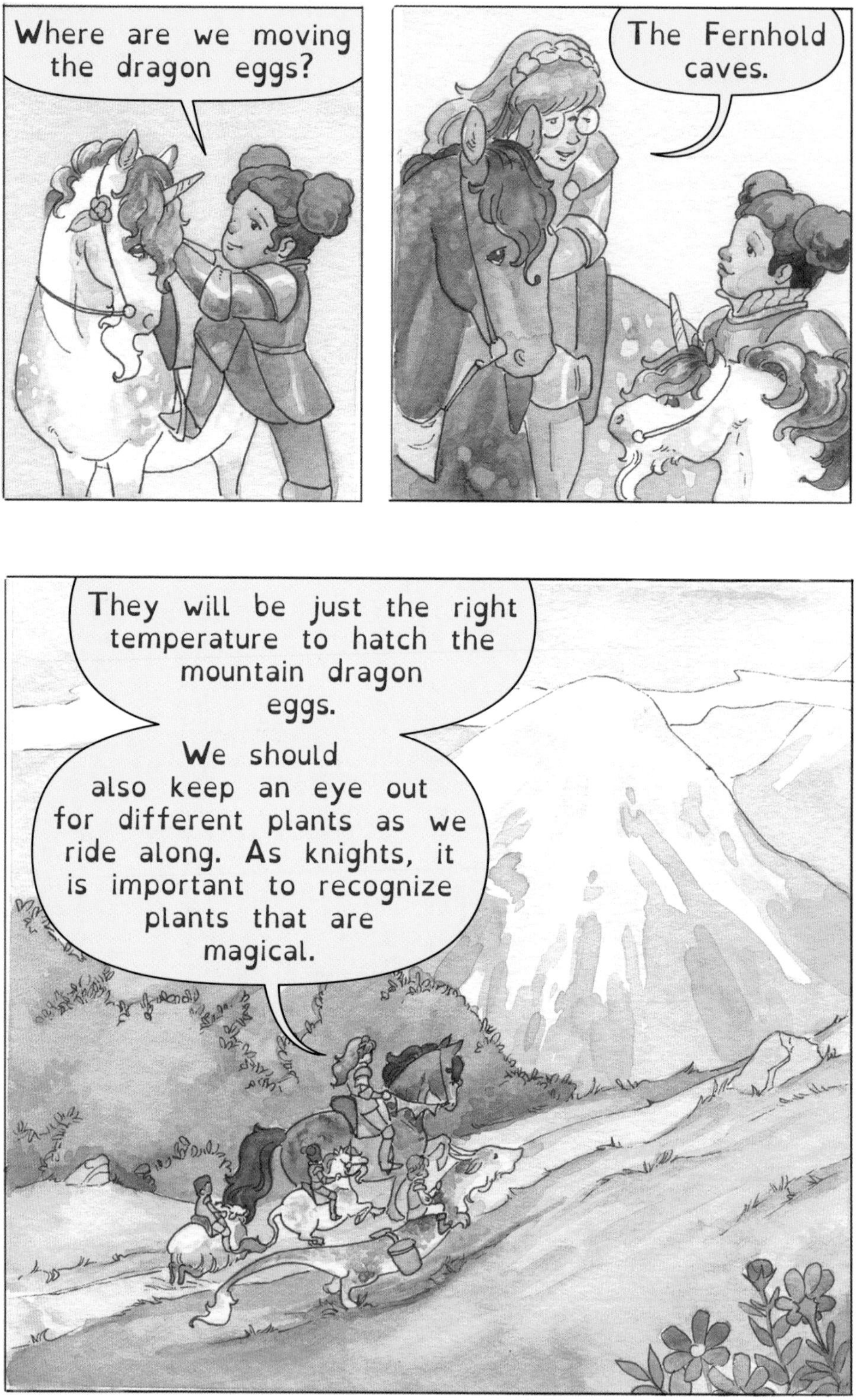

Where are we moving the dragon eggs?
The Fernhold caves.
They will be just the right temperature to hatch the mountain dragon eggs.
We should also keep an eye out for different plants as we ride along. As knights, it is important to recognize plants that are magical.

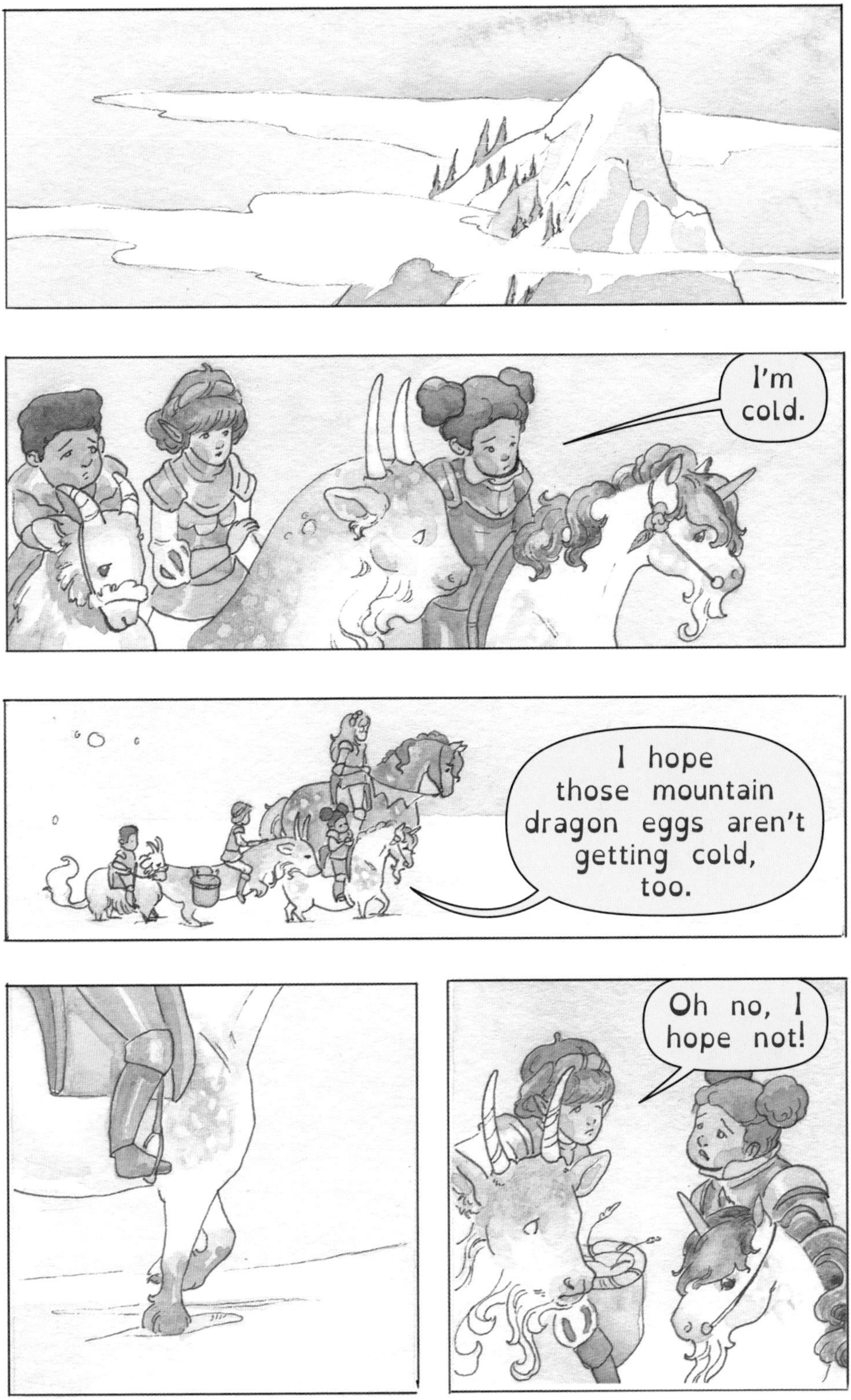
I'm cold.
I hope those mountain dragon eggs aren't getting cold, too.
Oh no, I hope not!

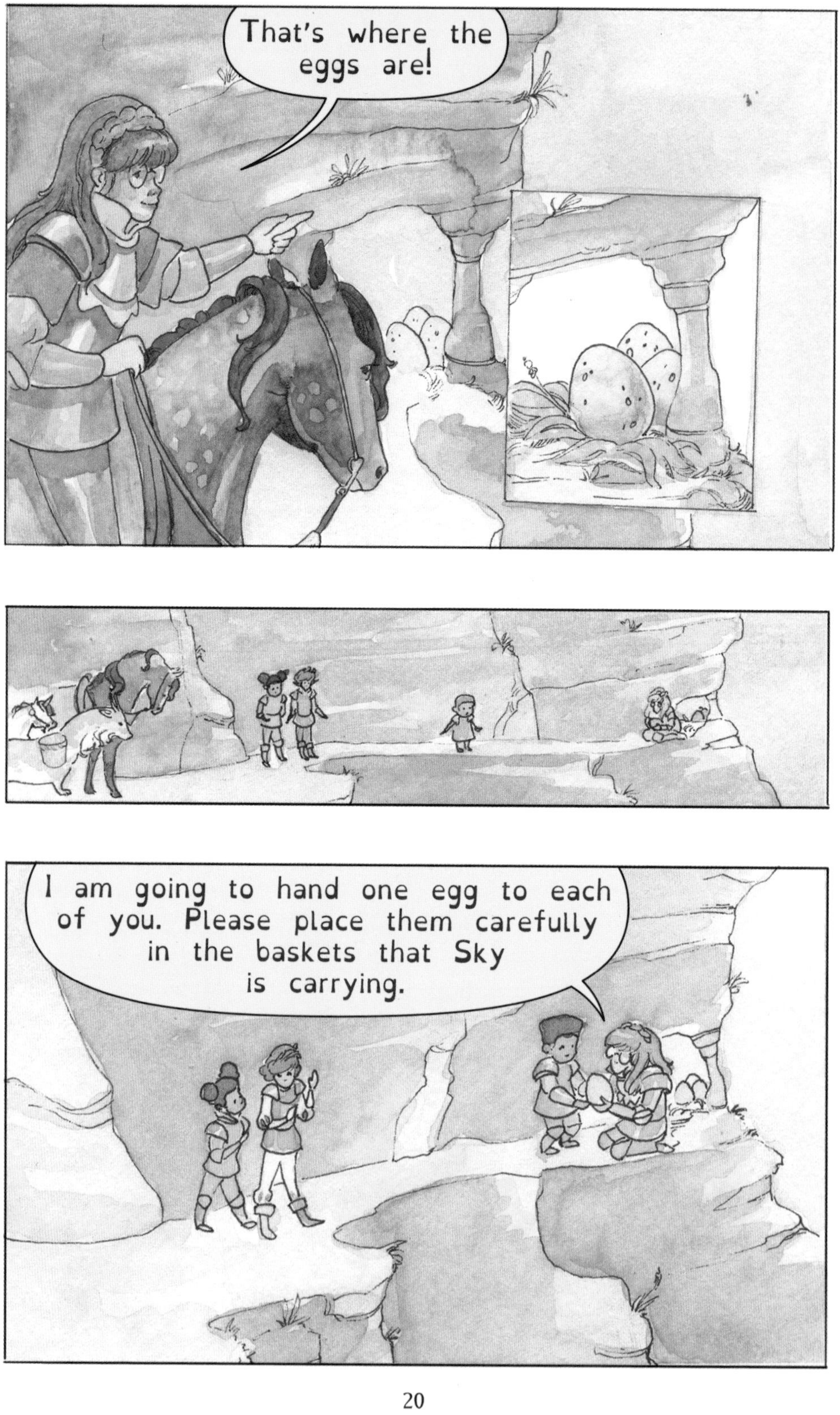
That's where the eggs are!
I am going to hand one egg to each of you. Please place them carefully in the baskets that Sky is carrying.

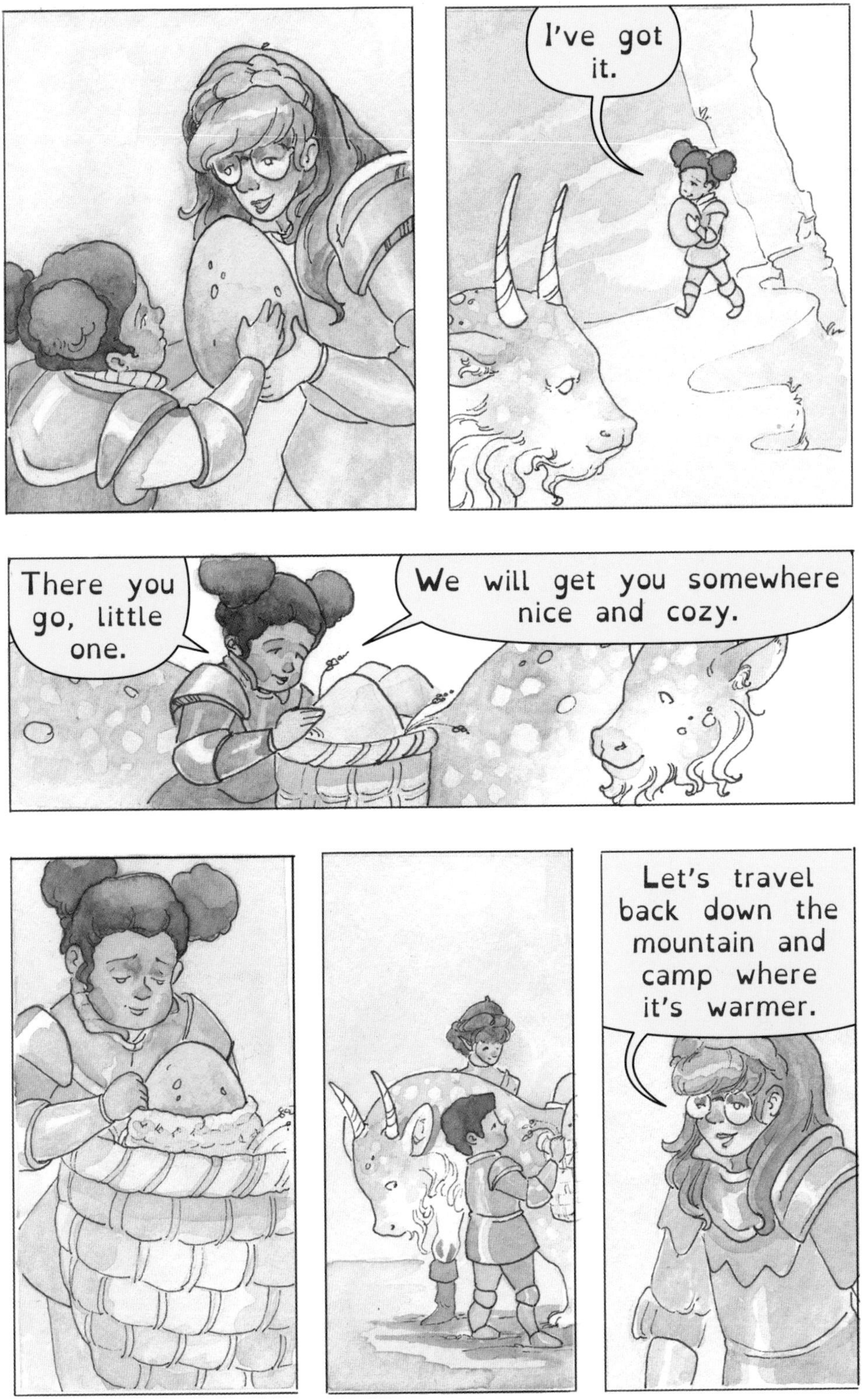
I've got it.
There you go, little one.
We will get you somewhere nice and cozy.
Let's travel back down the mountain and camp where it's warmer.

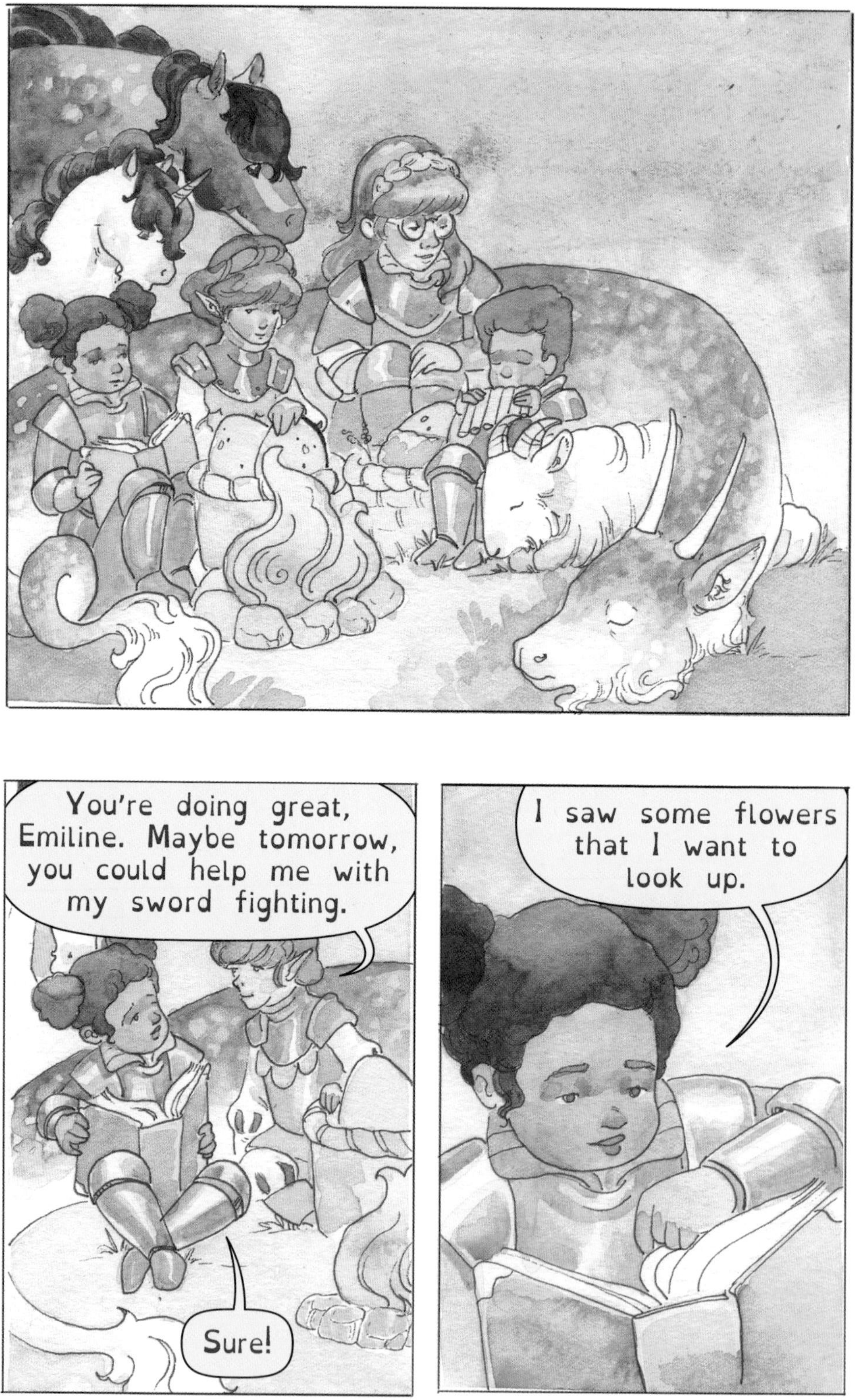
You're doing great, Emiline. Maybe tomorrow, you could help me with my sword fighting.
Sure!
I saw some flowers that I want to look up.

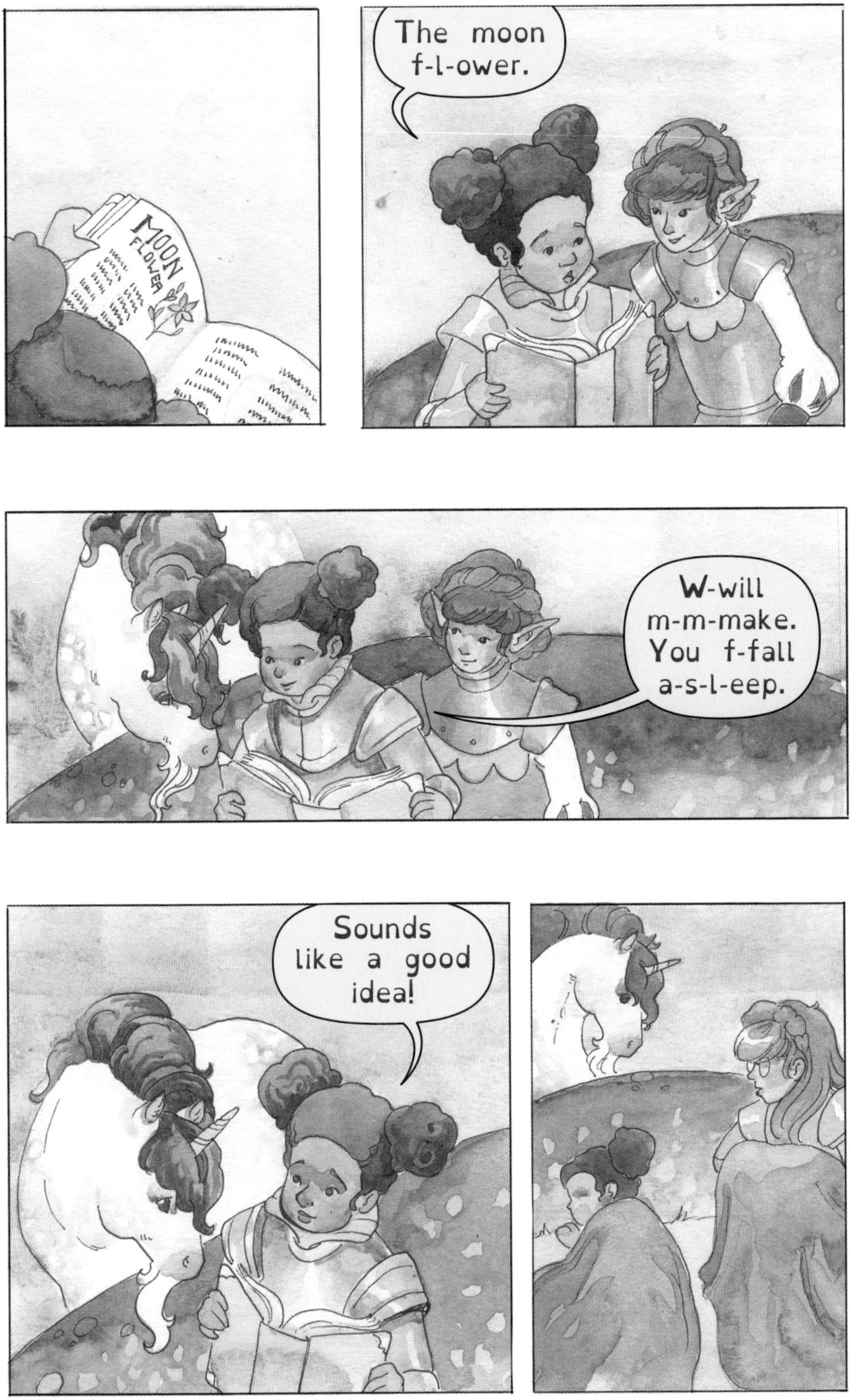
MOON FLOWER
The moon f-l-ower.
W-will m-m-make. You f-fall a-s-l-eep.
Sounds like a good idea!

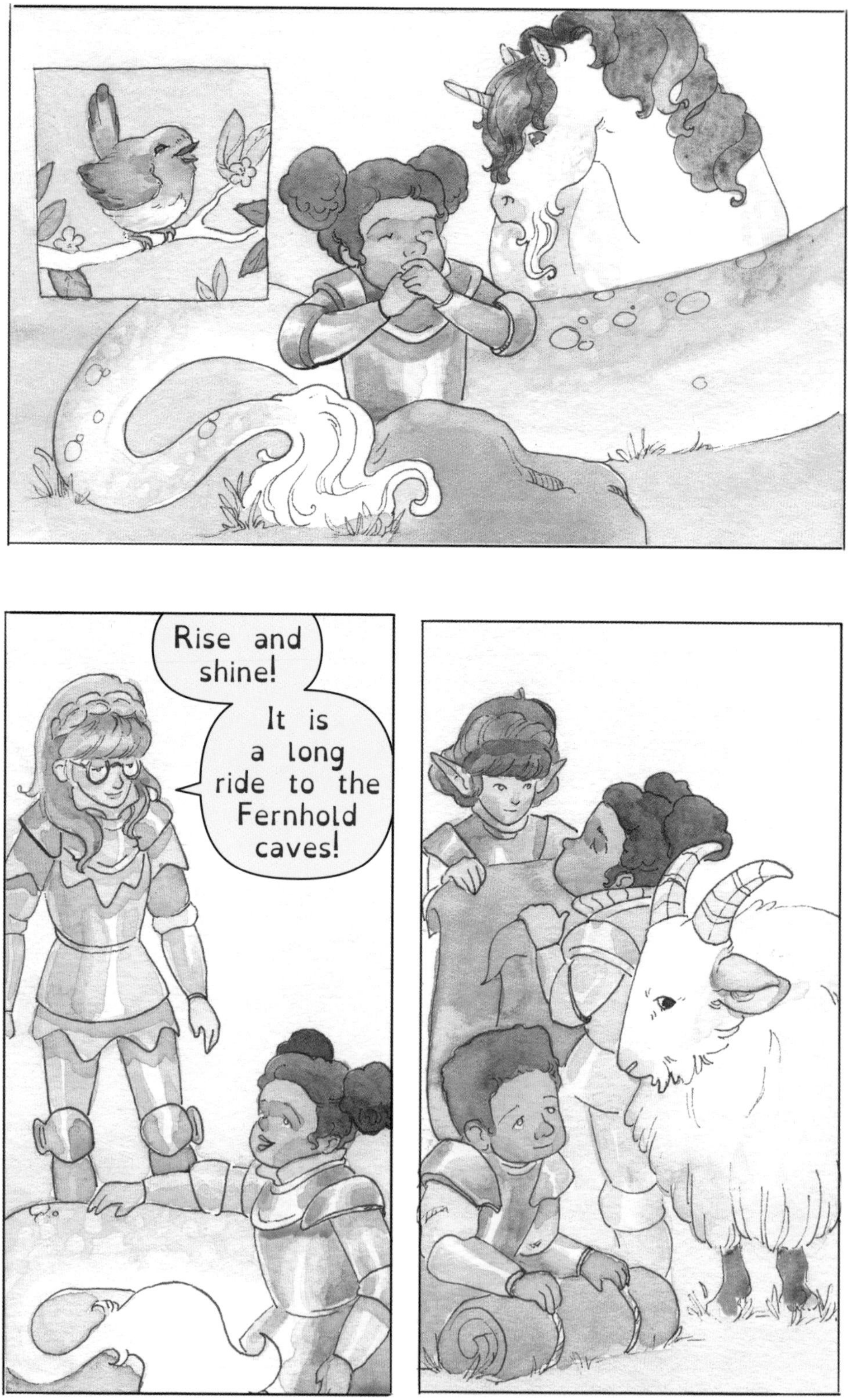
Rise and shine!
It is a long ride to the Fernhold caves!

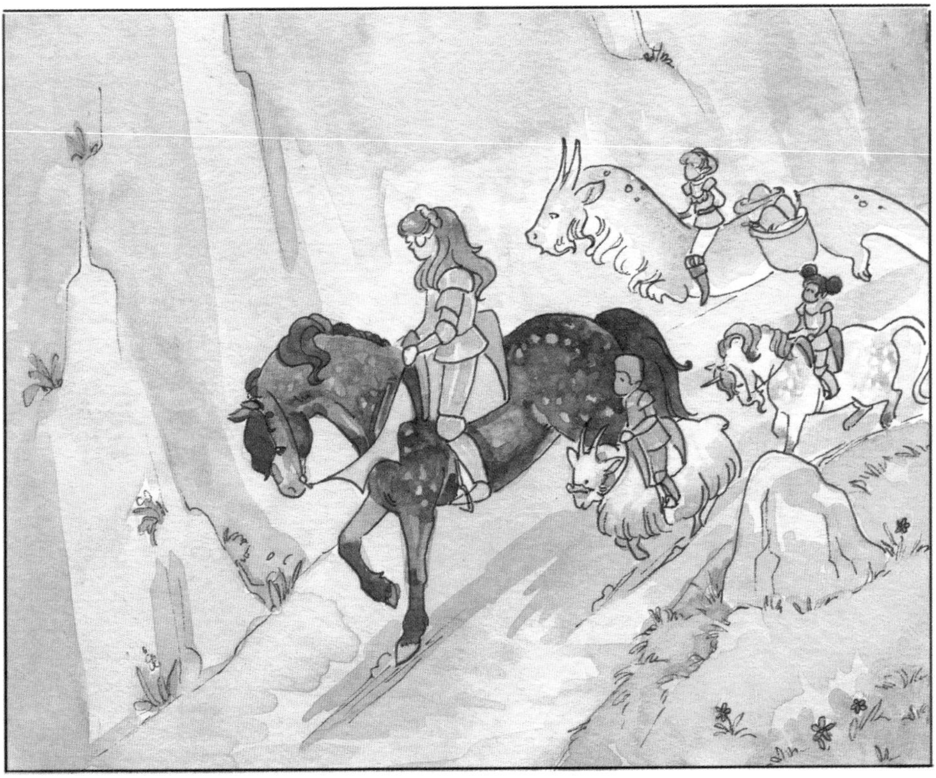

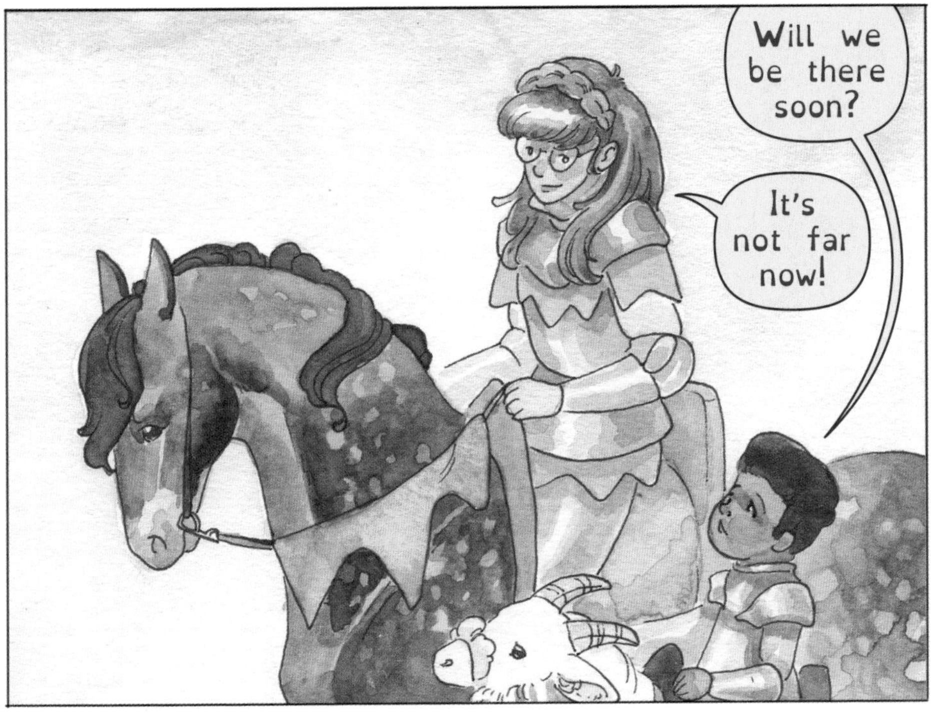
Will we be there soon?
It's not far now!

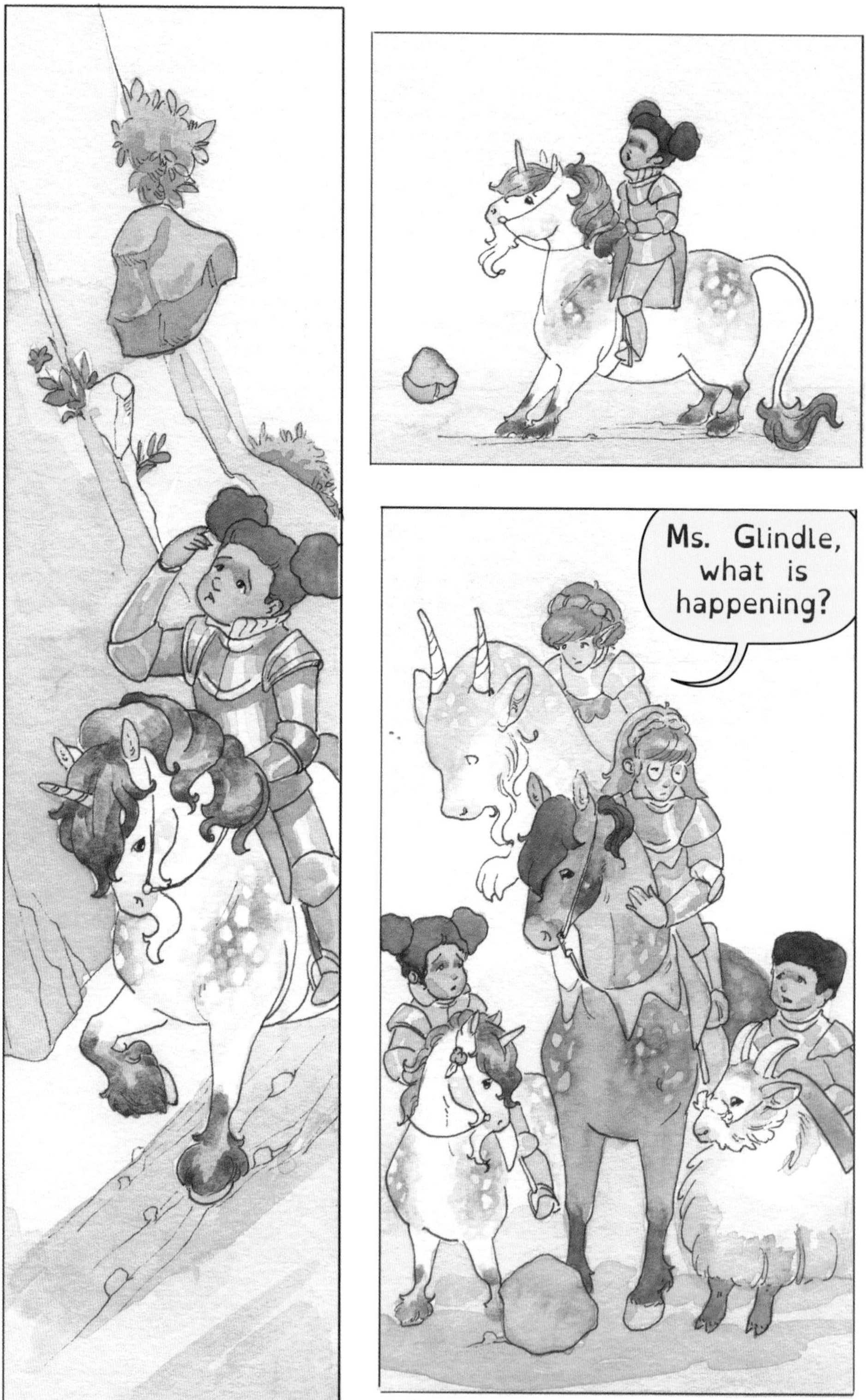
Ms. Glindle, what is happening?

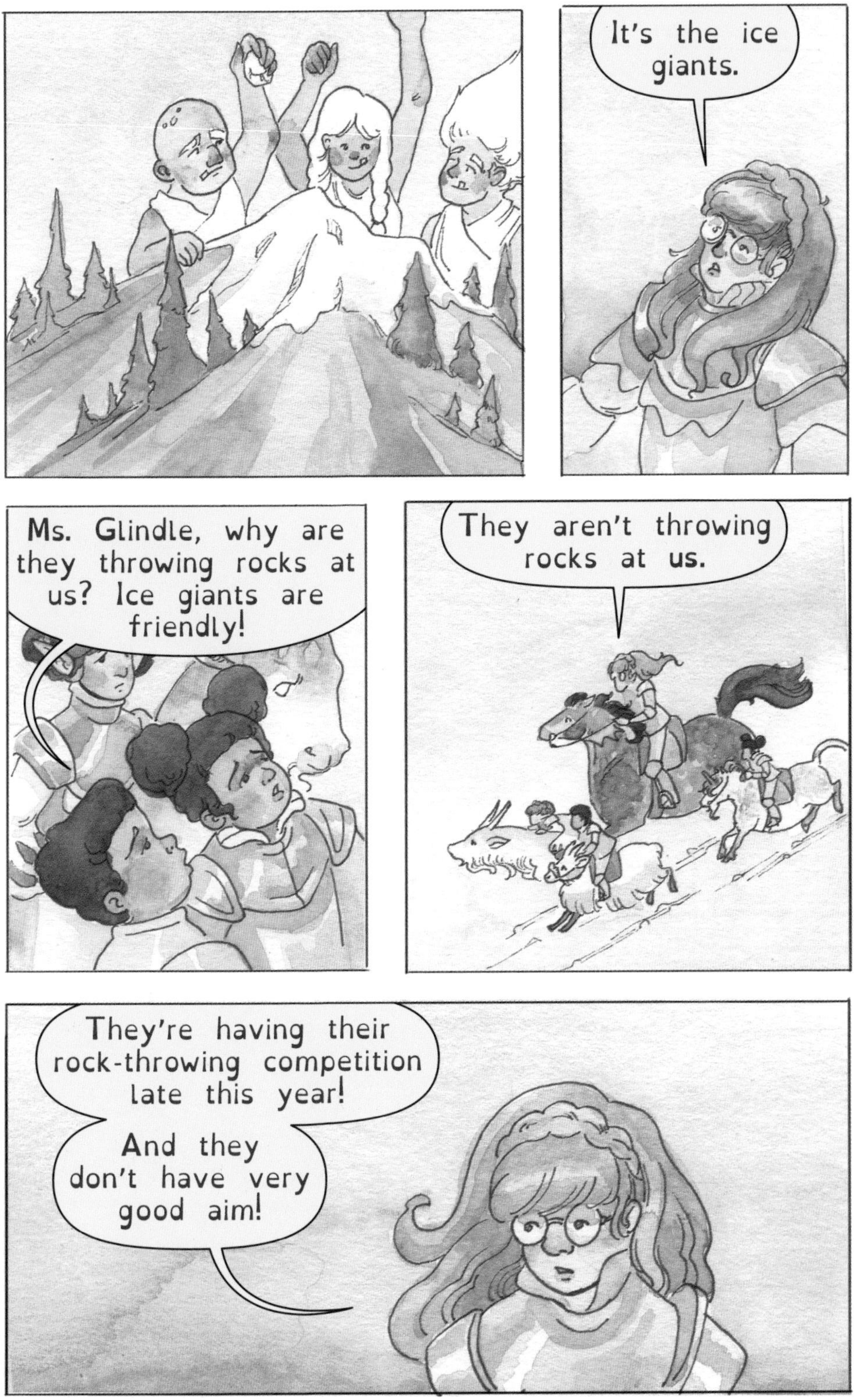
It's the ice giants.
Ms. Glindle, why are they throwing rocks at us? Ice giants are friendly!
They aren't throwing rocks at us.
They're having their rock-throwing competition late this year!
And they don't have very good aim!

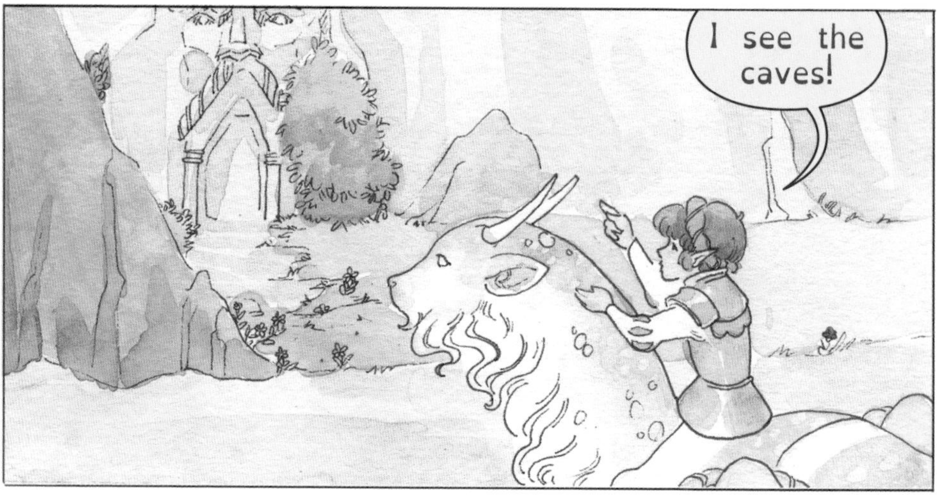
I see the caves!

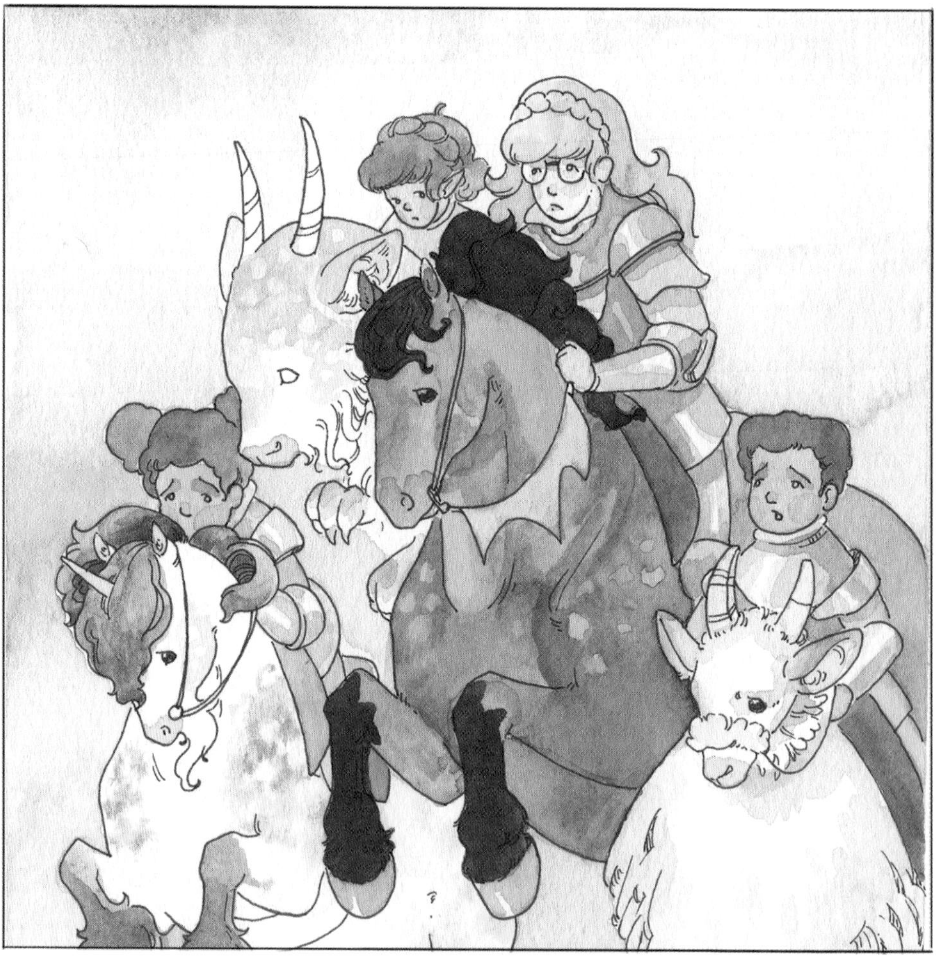

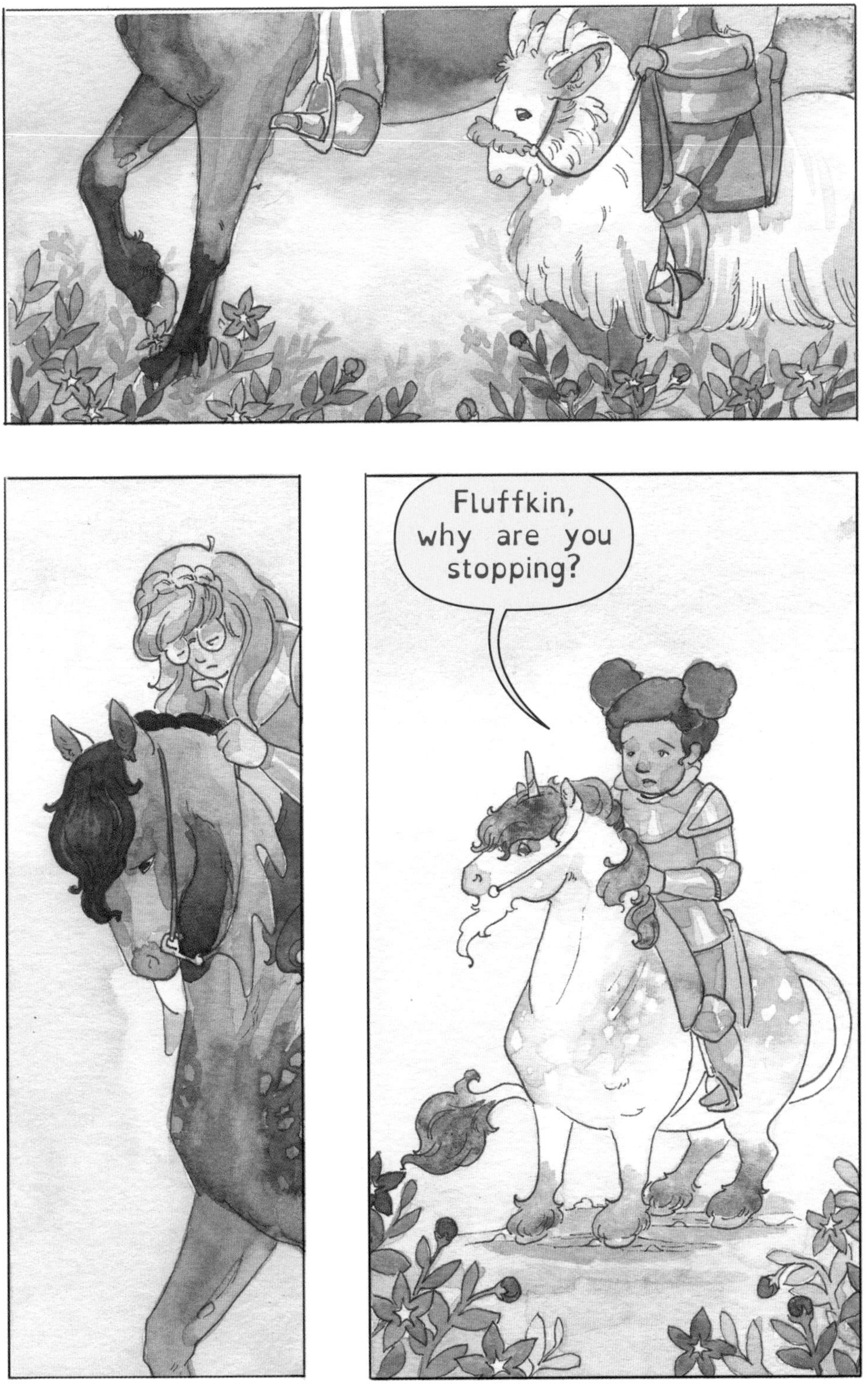
Fluffkin, why are you stopping?

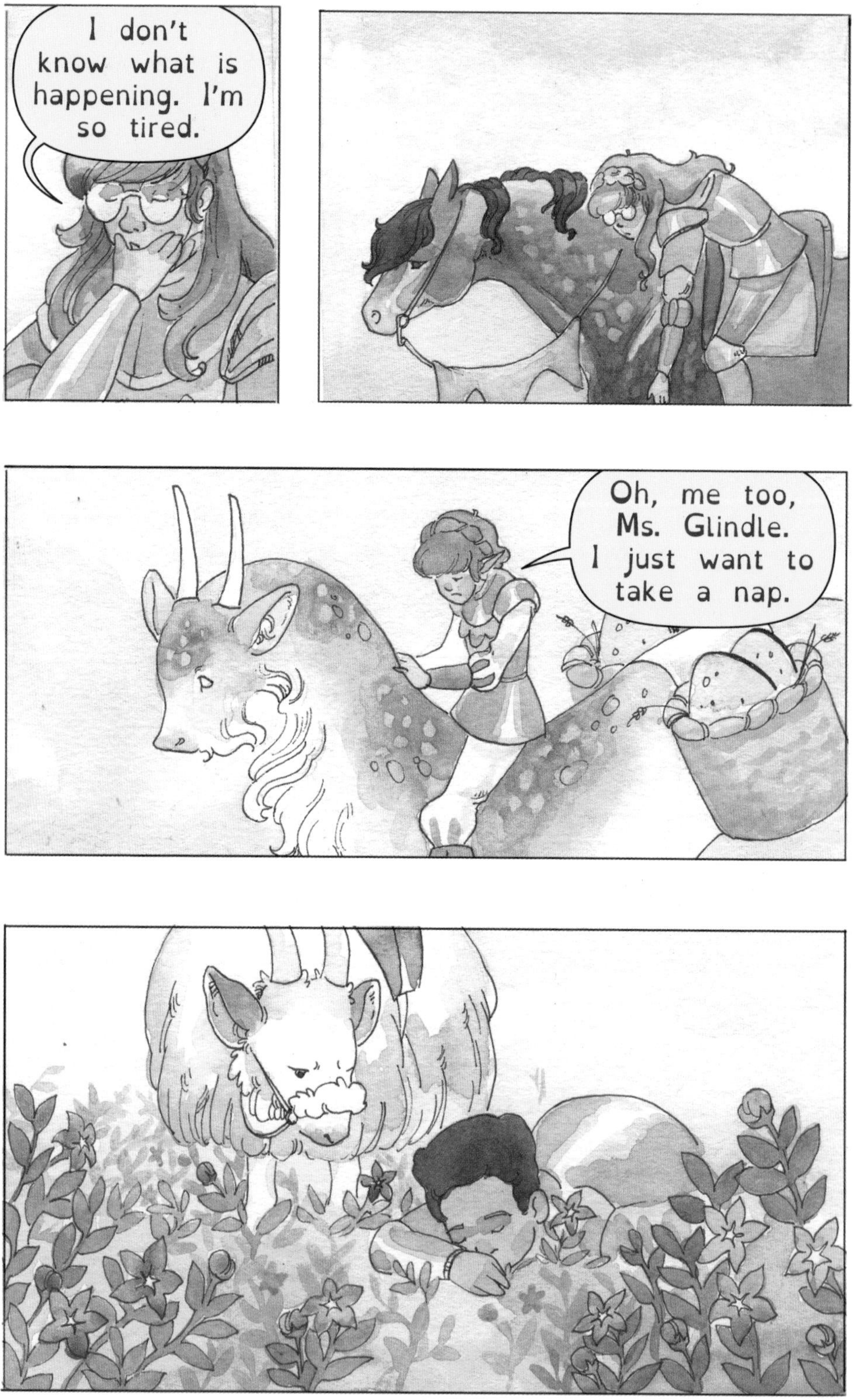
I don't know what is happening. I'm so tired.
Oh, me too, Ms. Glindle. I just want to take a nap.

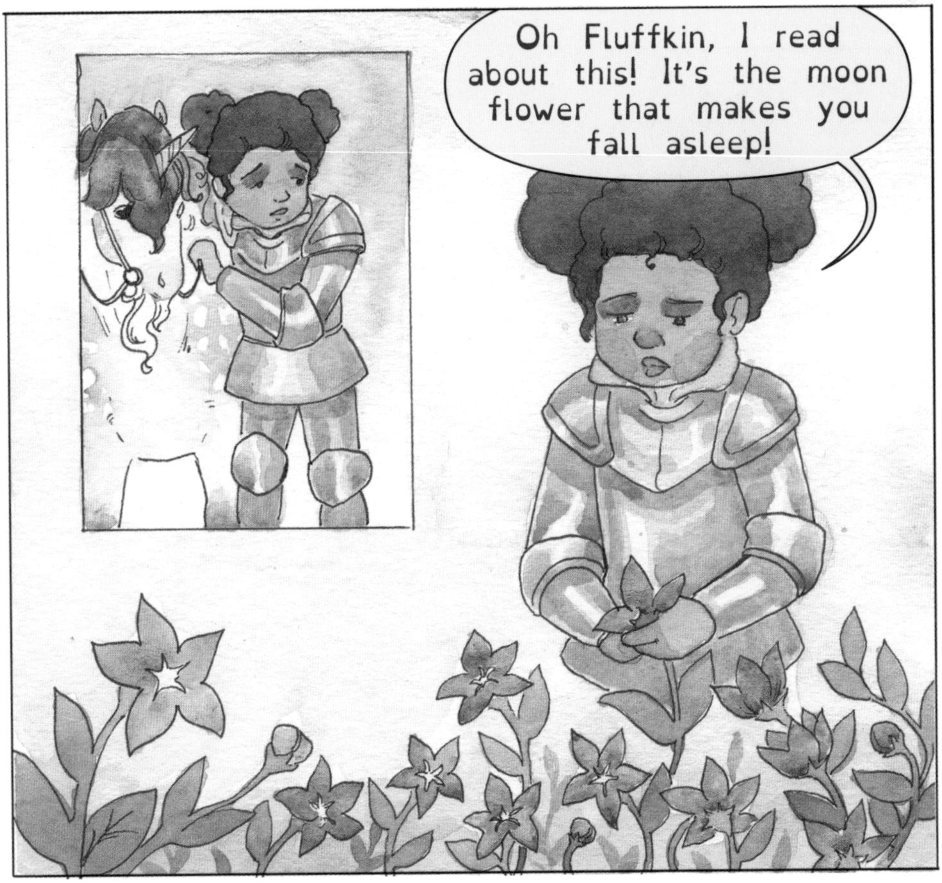
Oh Fluffkin, I read about this! It's the moon flower that makes you fall asleep!

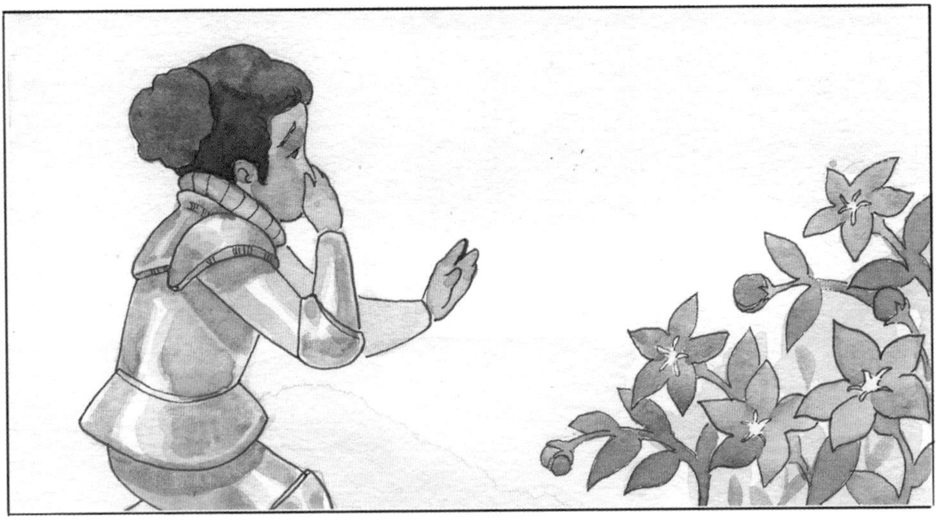

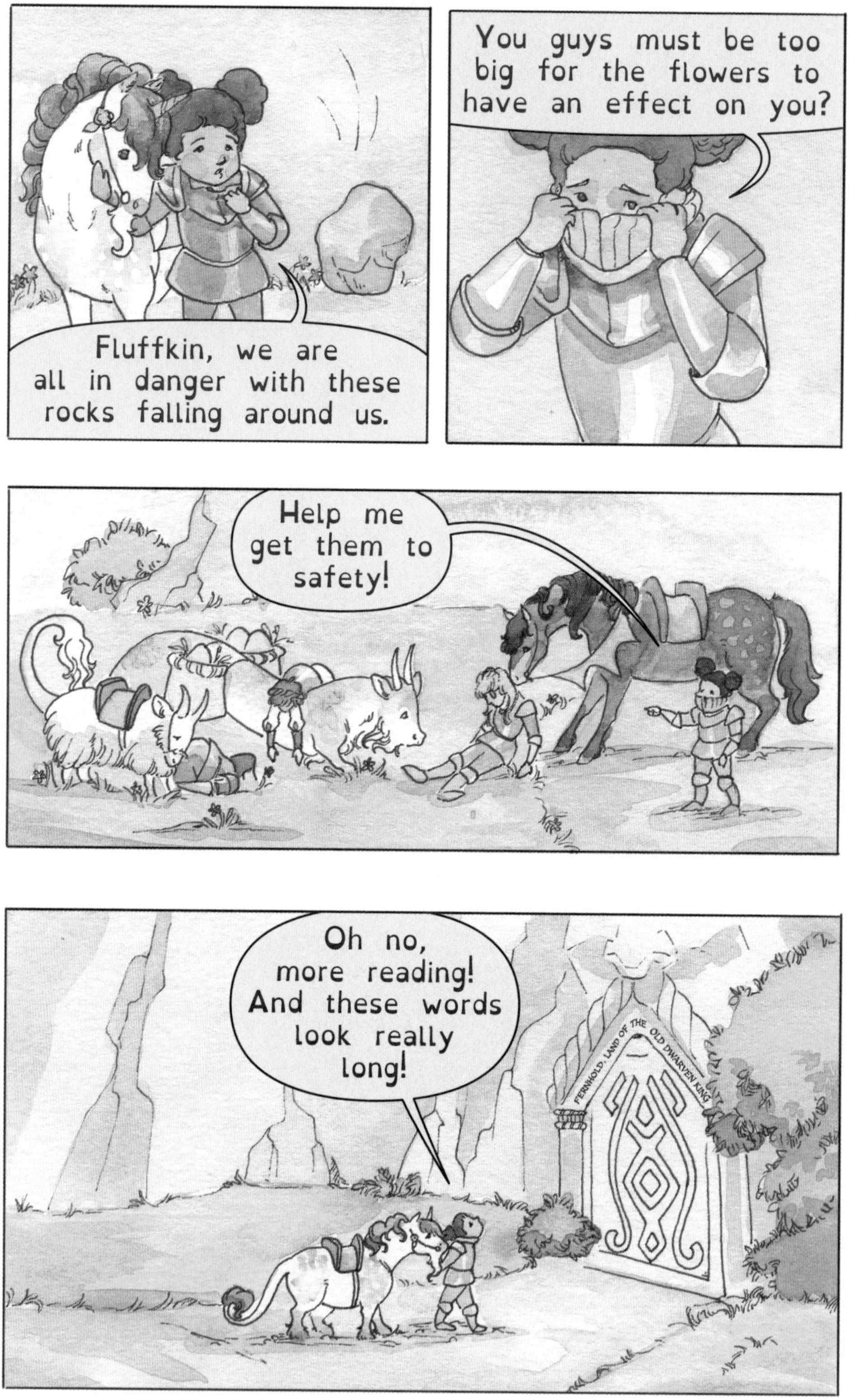
Fluffkin, we are all in danger with these rocks falling around us.
You guys must be too big for the flowers to have an effect on you?
Help me get them to safety!
Oh no, more reading! And these words look really long!
FERNHOLD, LAND OF THE OLD DWARVEN KING

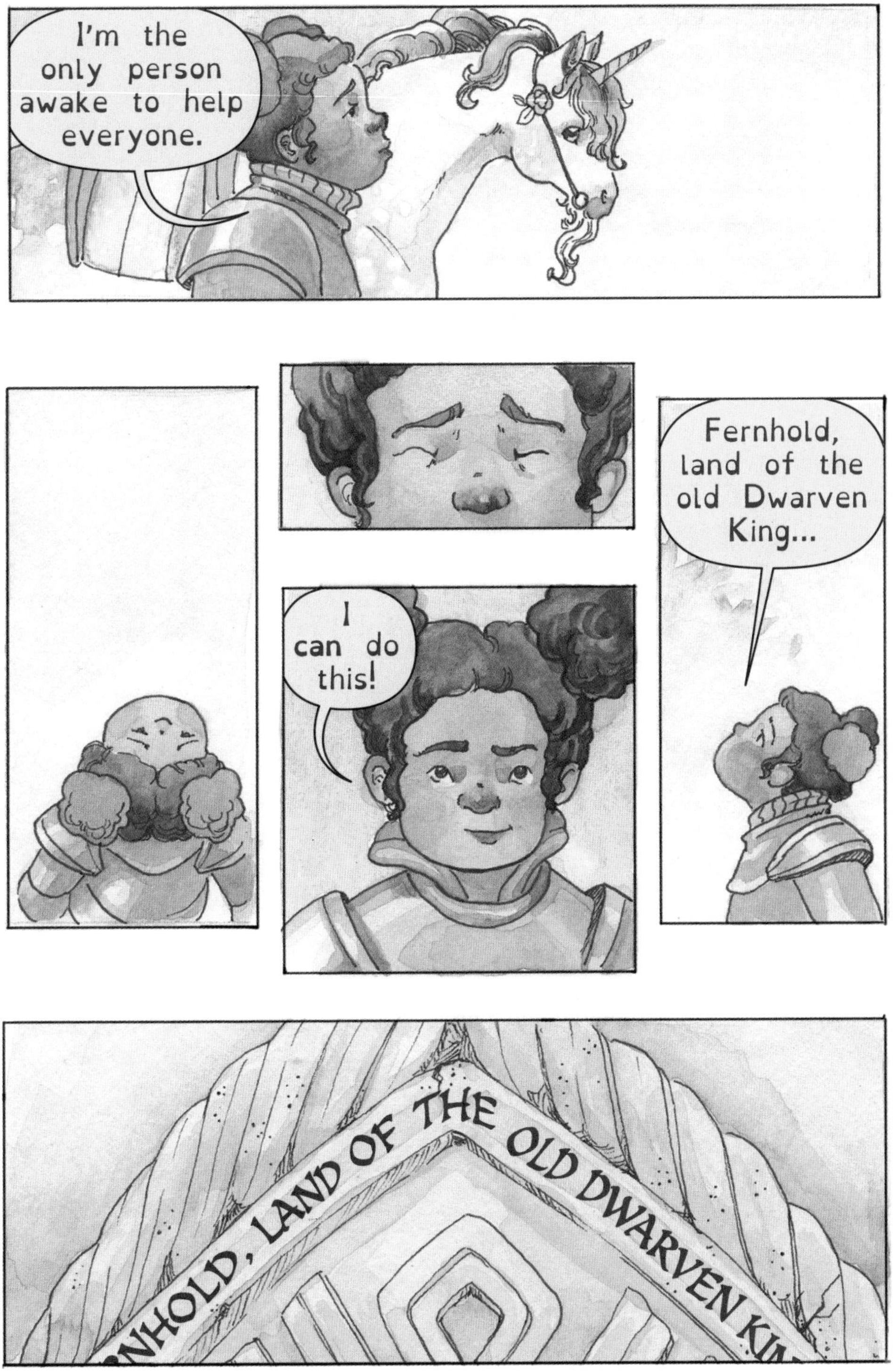
I'm the only person awake to help everyone.
I can do this!
Fernhold, land of the old Dwarven King...
NHOLD, LAND OF THE OLD DWARVEN KI

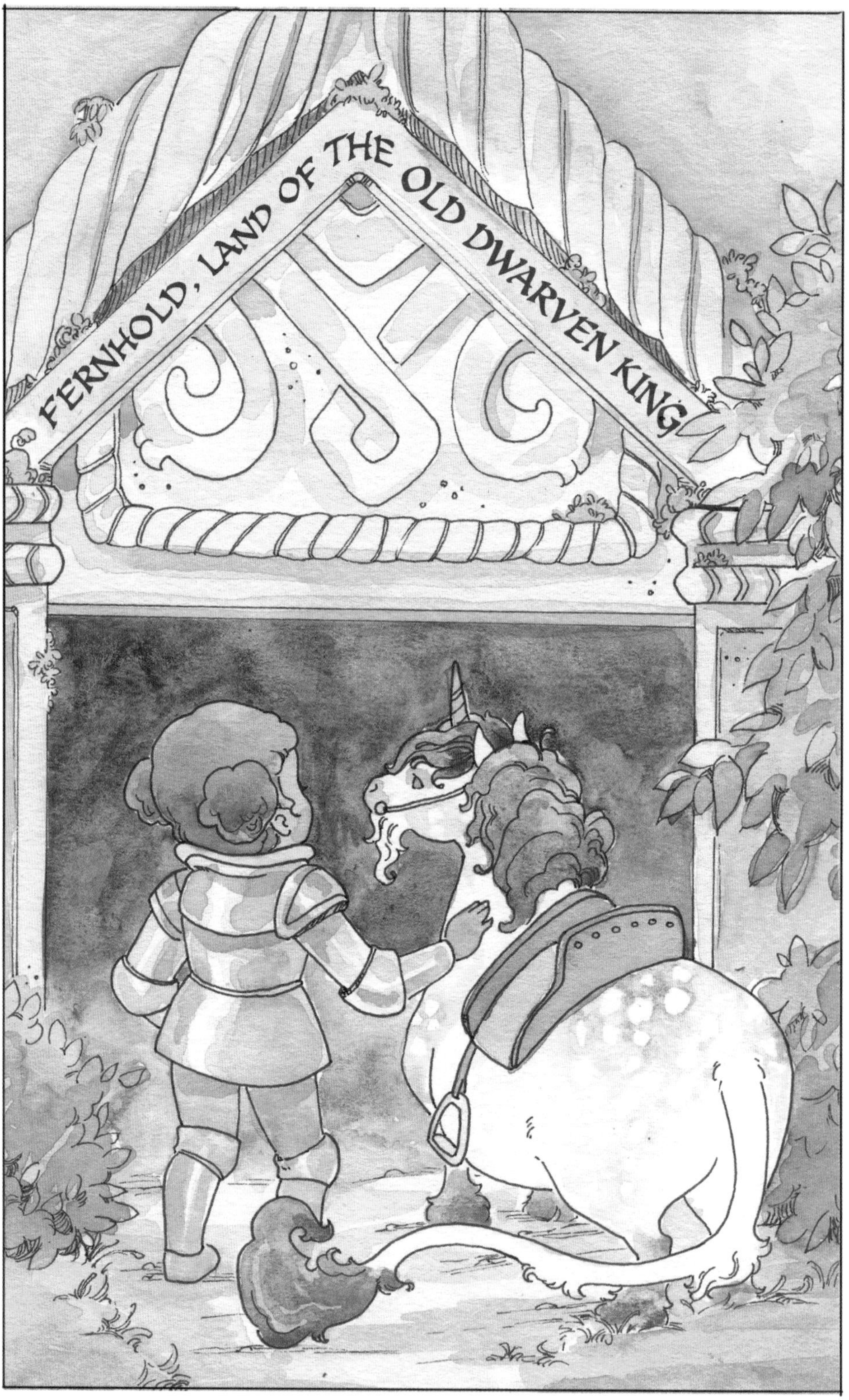
FERNHOLD, LAND OF THE OLD DWARVEN KING

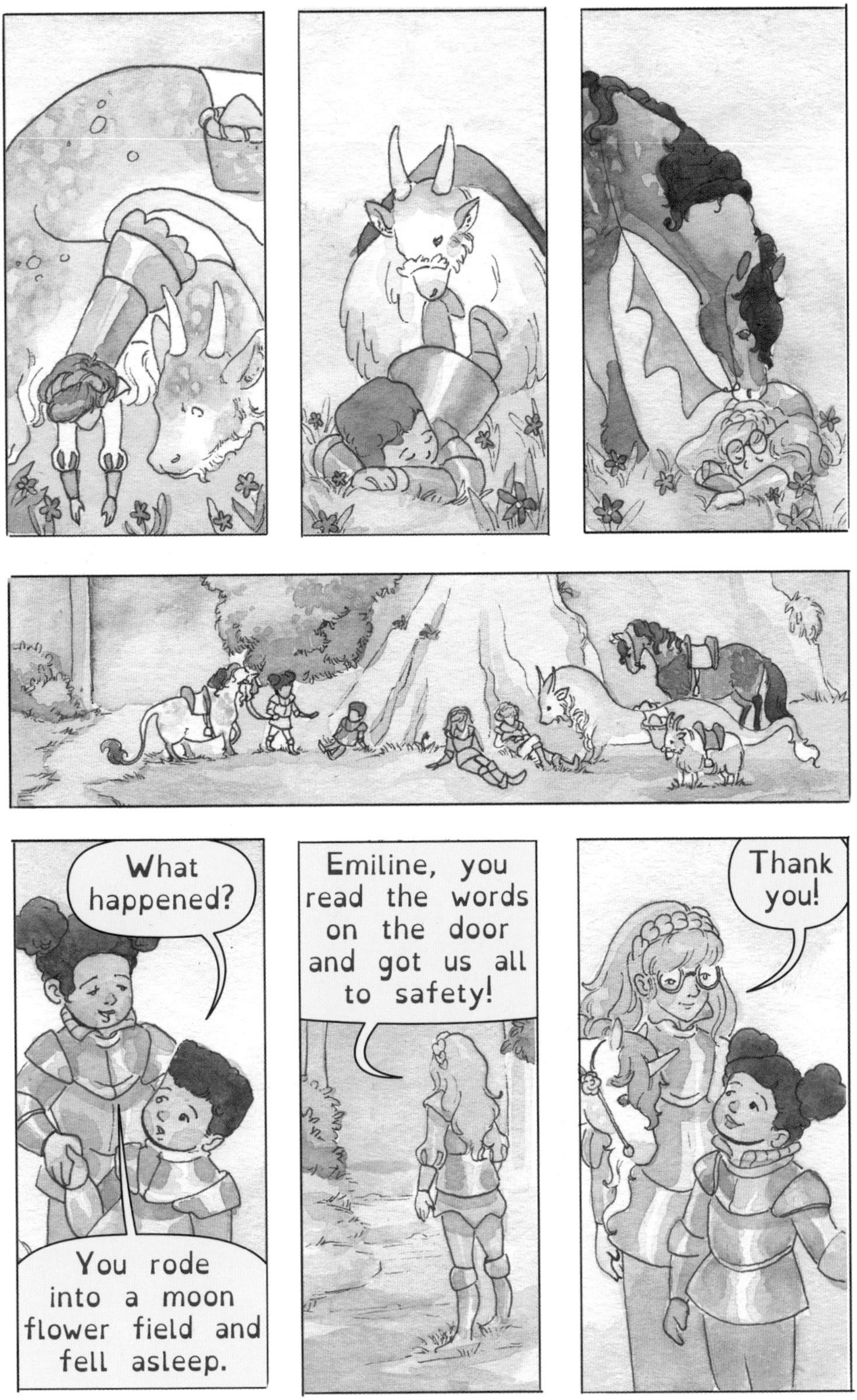
What happened?
You rode into a moon flower field and fell asleep.
Emiline, you read the words on the door and got us all to safety!
Thank you!

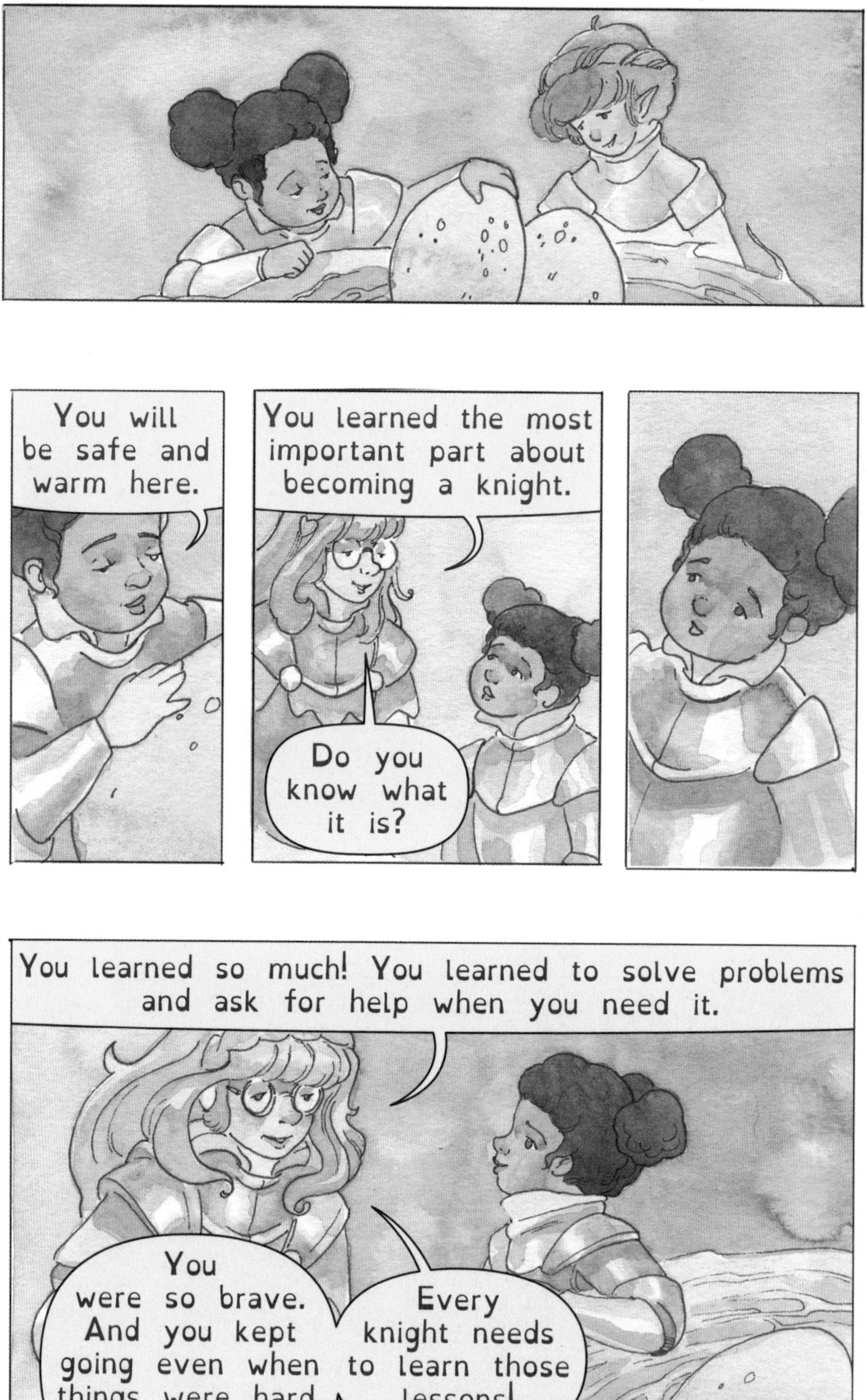
You will be safe and warm here.
You learned the most important part about becoming a knight.
Do you know what it is?
You learned so much! You learned to solve problems and ask for help when you need it.
You were so brave. And you kept going even when things were hard.
Every knight needs to learn those lessons!

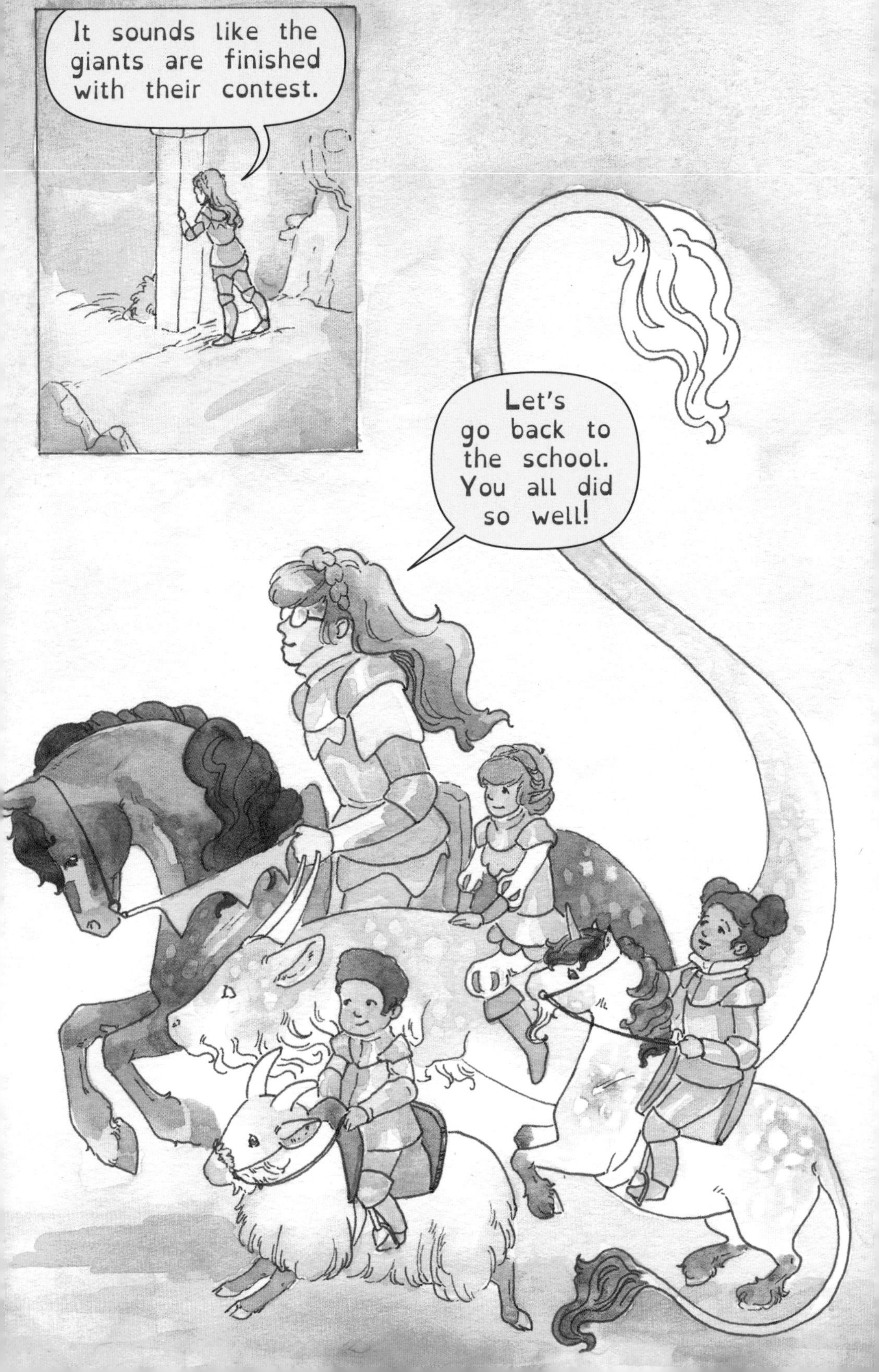
It sounds like the giants are finished with their contest.
Let's go back to the school. You all did so well!

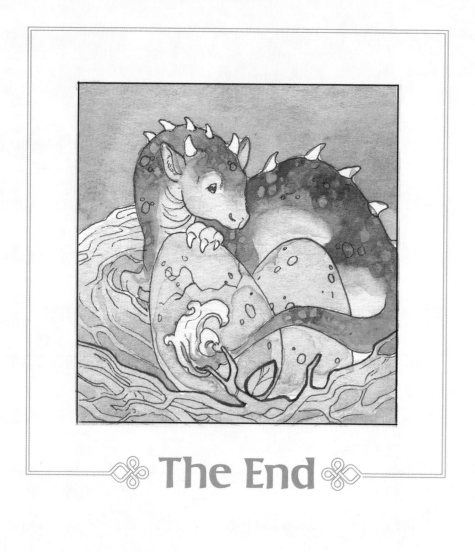

The End

Choose Your Steed!

Knights always have a trusty steed!
Which one is your favorite?

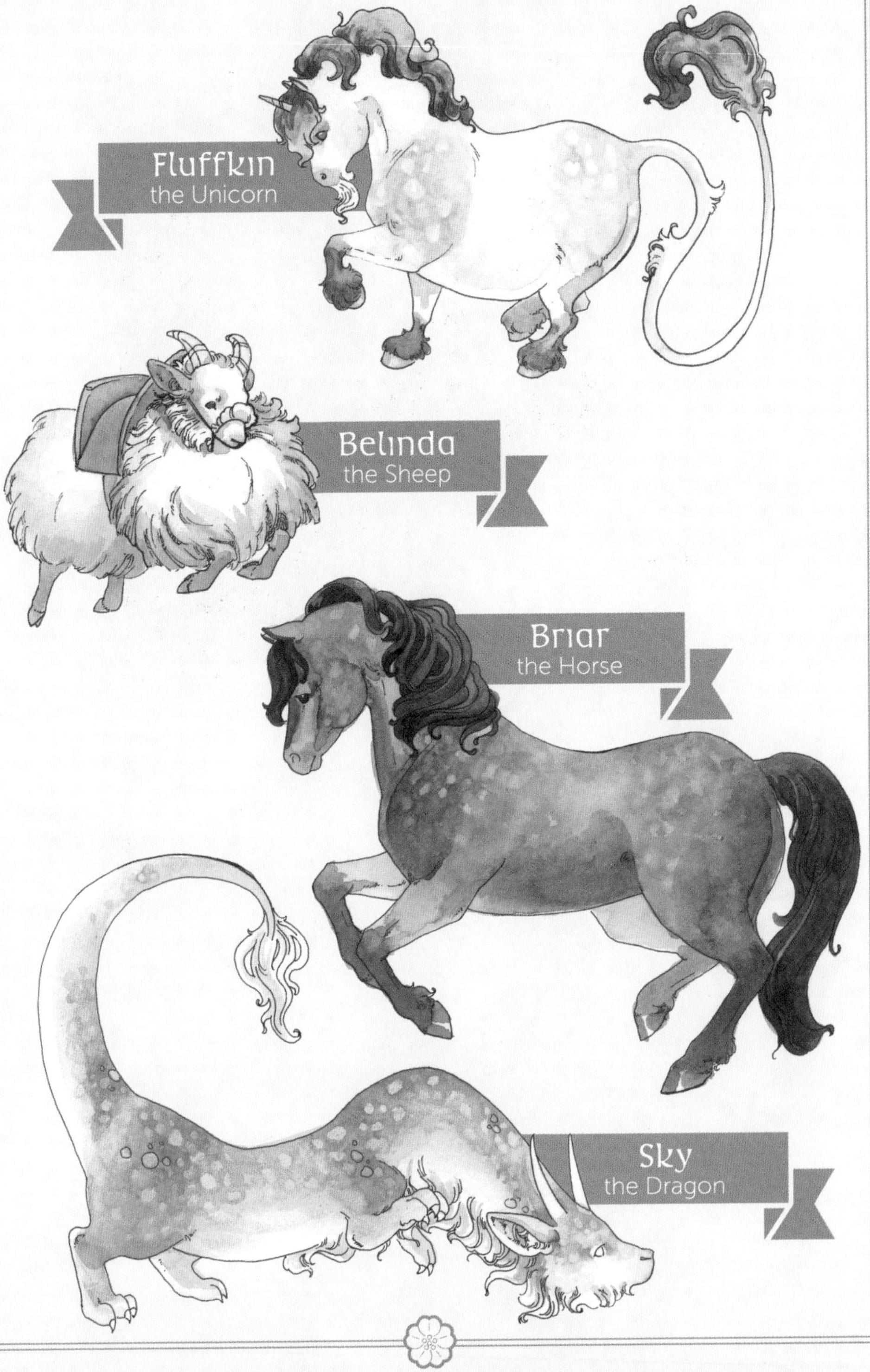
Fluffkin
the Unicorn
Belinda
the Sheep
Briar
the Horse
Sky
the Dragon

KIMBERLI has always loved to create stories and draw. When she was young, she always had new stories to tell, but writing them was difficult because she has dyslexia. Through hard work and the support of teachers and family, here she is creating comics for young readers.

Kimberli grew up and currently lives in what used to be the Wild West, with her cat, dog, and horse. She loves telling stories through art, drawing cute critters and magical folk.